HASSLE and the Medicine Man

OTHER BOOKS BY CLIFTON ADAMS

Stranger in Town

Reckless Men

The Dangerous Day of Kiowa Jones

Doomsday Creek

The Hottest Fourth of July in the History of Hangtree County

The Grabhorn Bounty

Shorty

A Partnership With Death

The Most Dangerous Profession

Tragg's Choice

The Last Days of Wolf Garnett

Biscuit-Shooter

The Badge and Harry Cole

Hard Times and Arnie Smith

Concannon

HASSLE and the Medicine Man

by Clifton Adams

DOUBLEDAY & COMPANY, INC.
Garden City, New York
1973

All of the characters in this book are fictitious,
and any resemblance to actual persons,
living or dead, is purely coincidental.

ISBN: 0-385-02889-X
Library of Congress Catalog Card Number 72-89289

Printed in the United States of America
First Edition

1

CALIFORNIA SAM—that Benefactor of Mankind, the Toast of European Royalty, not to mention Envy of the Greatest Scientific Minds of the Age—had been felled by an infirmity that defied even his own acknowledged genius. He had a hangover. Possibly the great-grandfather of all hangovers. When he tried sitting on the edge of his bed the room began to spin. His stomach rushed to his throat. His vision blurred.

There was a light knocking at his door.

California Sam ignored it. He lay like a dead man, oblivious to all but the most painful bedbug bites and the lurching of his stomach. There was another light rapping. "Go away," the great man groaned. He fell into a fitful sleep.

As if from a great distance, Sam heard the door open. A young male voice said, "I brought you some coffee from downstairs."

"Whoever you are," the White Wa-Hoe Medicine Man gasped weakly, "get out of my room. I don't want any coffee." He drifted off on a rolling sea of unconsciousness.

A blinding slant of sunshine filtered through the room's solitary window and fell across the face of the World's Foremost Authority on the Savage Wa-Hoe Indians. He groaned, shaded his eyes and stared at the young boy who was watching him from the foot of the bed.

Very carefully, California Sam pushed himself out of the sun's blinding glare and sat on the edge of the bed. "Who are you, boy?" he asked with absolutely no interest.

"Hassle Jones," the boy said gravely. "You said wake you first thing this mornin'."

"Why did I want you to wake me?" Sam asked dully, running a furry tongue around the inside of his mouth.

The boy grinned. "You said you aimed to pull out at first light."

The medicine man shuddered. It was all coming back now—very dimly. He had made the Wa-Hoe Electric Hair Restorer pitch, and the Wichita yokels, like yokels everywhere, had grabbed up the little jars of magic salve as fast as Sam could take their money. A first-class pitch it had been. He remembered fondly. But there was one thing to keep in mind when dealing in electric hair restorers—it was never wise to linger long in a place after making the pitch.

The boy regarded him with interest. "Wake you up, you said. Bring coffee. You'd give me a half a dollar, you said. On top of the other half a dollar you was goin' to give me for riggin' your torches."

"I said that?"

"Yes sir. And you said you'd take me with you when you pulled out."

"I think I'll have a go at that coffee, after all." Sam groaned. He took the cup in a shaking hand and regarded it doubtfully. It was bitter and gritty and black as the heart of a Denver policeman. He drank a little of it and was immediately sorry. What I need, he told himself with no nonsense, is a real drink. "Hand me my pants," he told the boy.

Young Hassle Jones handed him his pants, which were of creamy buckskin, with fancy buckskin fringe along the outside seams. Sam sat in his union suit, abstractedly going through his pockets. The pockets were empty. A profound sadness looked out of the great man's bloodshot eyes. Without any real hope, he said to the boy, "Hand me my coat."

The boy handed him his coat, which was also of elaborately fringed buckskin to match the pants. The coat pockets were empty. All his money—in the neighborhood of forty dollars—was gone. Also his real diamond stickpin, his fake diamond-cut glass ring, his stem-wound watch and silver pocketknife. Everything gone.

He dimly remembered a redheaded saloon woman and several bottles of champagne wine. A real fandango! Never let it be said that California Sam was close with his money when he had it. But it was a cruel blow to his pride that a man of his experience had been cleaned out by a common saloon woman. It was humiliating.

Breathing heavily, Sam got into his shirt and pulled on his pants. He lunged up from the bed and quickly splashed his face at the washstand. For some moments he stared at himself in the looking glass. It was not a sight to inspire confidence.

The only sound in the room was the wheezing of the medicine man's breathing. With morbid fascination he stared at his long, hound-dog face in the glass. It showed with steel-etched clarity the ravages of fifty years of free and easy living. He could imagine that the grime of a thousand pitchman's torches was ground into his skin, along with the smell of aloe and cheap soap-making perfumes. Sam, he told that hard-used face in the looking glass, you've got to find yourself a new pitch; you're gettin' too old for this kind of livin'.

To the boy he said, "What did you say your name was?"

"Hassle Jones," the youth told him.

"How old are you, Hassle?"

"Eleven. Twelve next December."

"Well, Hassle, eleven's pretty old. Almost a man. Do you figger you're old enough to take disappointment like a man?"

The boy looked at him with hostility. "You ain't goin' to give me the dollar you owe me."

"Son," Sam told him in his roundest, most fatherly tones, "there ain't nothin' that would give me more pleasure right now than to hand you over the dollar. But the cruel truth is I ain't got it. I was robbed last night by a redheaded saloon woman by the name of Rose McGee. It's right humiliatin' to admit, but she cleaned me out as slick as a high pitchman cleanin' the greenest yokel in Iowa. Not that I aim to let her get away with it, mind you. Hand me my hat."

Scowling, the boy picked up the wide-brim beaver hat and handed it to him. "I know Rose," he said sternly. "She's been good to me. She wouldn't do a thing like that."

Sam settled the hat on his throbbing head. "Boy, you've got a lot of things to learn about women. And I'm afraid your education won't come cheap."

"I want my dollar."

"You'll get it. You've got the word of California Sam hisself on that. Now you just do like I tell you and pretty soon we'll have the whole business settled."

"Do what?"

"In just a minute I'm goin' to walk out of this room. I want you to stay behind for a while. I aim to walk outside the hotel and stand below this window. When everything's set I'll whistle a few bars of 'Dixie,' and when you hear it I want you to drop my valise out of the window. You understand?"

The youth looked at him coolly. "You aim to beat the hotel out of *their* money."

Sam gasped indignantly. "Boy, beatin' the hotel is the very last thing in my mind. That would be dishonest. Do I look like the kind of man that would welch on an honest debt?" Wisely, he hurried on without giving the boy a chance to answer. "The truth is, I was up a little late last night. I don't feel so good. If I was to walk out of here right now, with my valise in my hand, why there'd most likely be a row with the desk clerk. And a row is one thing I don't want just at this minute. You can understand that, can't you?"

"I still think you aim to beat the hotel."

California Sam looked as if he had just been stabbed in the back by his best friend. He shook his aching head sorrowfully. "Boy, you got to learn to *trust* people. Now I'm goin' out to tend to a little business. Then I'll come back and settle with the hotel, everything fair and square. I'll settle with you, too. You want that dollar, don't you?"

"What do you want with your valise, if you aim to come back?"

"You hurt me, boy." Sam tapped his chest on the left side to show just where the pain was. "I want my valise because that's where my medicine is. Medicine's my stock in trade—I got to have it to raise the money for you and the hotel."

Hassle could think of no immediate argument to that. He did know for a fact that California Sam was a medicine show doc and that medicine was his business. Reluctantly, he said, "How long you want me to wait here?"

"Just till I come back. It shouldn't take long to get my business settled with a certain Miss McGee." As he was going out of the door, Sam reminded him, "Don't forget. When you hear 'Dixie' just let my valise out of the window."

Hassle sat on the edge of the bed and waited. From the open window he could hear the town of Wichita stirring in the early morning sun. Wagons rattled by in the dusty street. From the distant shipping pens he could hear the cattle bawling.

"I wish I was in de land ob cotton . . ."

The whistled notes of "Dixie" drifted clearly up to the window of the hotel room. Still dubious about the whole business, the boy lifted the medicine man's valise to the window ledge and let it drop.

At his station beneath the window, California Sam caught the valise with a careless ease that suggested a great deal of practice in such exercises. He hitched at his pants and sauntered off toward Omar's Western Trail Saloon.

The bartender of the Western Trail took one look at the long-faced bird in the fancy buckskins and casually ran his hand along a lower shelf, feeling for a bung starter. He had seen that look before. The self-righteousness. The indignity. The look of a man whose pride had been shattered almost beyond repair.

The medicine man leaned on the bar and sized the barkeep up with his bloodshot eyes. He knew exactly what the bartender was thinking. He knew what the unseen hand was doing on the bottom shelf. "I'm lookin' for a lady," he said, "by the name of McGee. A redheaded lady, and not too hard lookin', the best I can recall. I want to talk to her about a matter of business."

"She ain't here," the bartender told him, taking a firm grip on the bung starter.

"Maybe you can tell me where to find her," said California Sam.

"I don't know where you can find her. What she does when she ain't workin' ain't none of my business."

The medicine man heaved a sigh. He moved down the bar to where several heavy beer mugs were neatly stacked. He picked up one and regarded it with affection. "Now," he went on, "you don't have to tell me anything of course, if you don't want to. You can haul out that bung starter and commence the fandango. And I'll fling this beer mug and most likely cause considerable damage to your mirror.

Then the town marshal will come and there'll be hell to pay all around. I'll wind up in the calaboose, and you'll be out two hundred dollars for a new mirror. What good will that do anybody?"

The barkeep paled. "Put that mug down! Are you loco?"

"I just want to talk to Miss Rose McGee."

The man picked up a bar rag and patted his sweaty forehead. "Like I told you, Rose ain't here. She lives at the Kansas House—that's a hotel, kind of. If she ain't there, I don't know where she is."

"Much oblige for your help," Sam said pleasantly, putting the mug down on the bar.

He walked outside and stood on the plankwalk for a while, regarding the angle of the July sun. He judged the time at about nine o'clock. Being without a watch, that was the best he could do.

He heaved a heavy, regretful sigh at the thought of what probably lay ahead. Women had no sense of propriety. They were highly excitable creatures for the most part, Sam had found. They tended to become hysterical under stress, particularly when they were threatened with the loss of something of value—even when the thing of value didn't belong to them.

In his present condition Sam would have gladly overlooked the loss of his money, ring, watch, and knife. They weren't worth making a racket about. Besides, it was embarrassing to go to a woman like that and admit that she had outfoxed him. But the diamond stickpin was an entirely different matter. In palmier days he had paid seven hundred dollars for that stickpin. It was his insurance against disaster of one sort or another that forever haunted the trail of a pitchman, and he was entirely against the notion of having that insurance canceled by the likes of Rose McGee.

"Nothin' for it, old son," he told himself sadly. "You got

to hunt her down and, by hook or by crook, get back that stickpin."

He found the Kansas House near that unmarked boundary that had, in earlier, wilder times, been spoken of as the "deadline." But this was July 1894 and the days of the big cattle drives were all but forgotten. The Kansas House which, no doubt, had known livelier times, now looked quiet and slightly bored, like the town itself. California Sam stepped up to the front porch and put his head in the open doorway.

A small, birdlike woman was in the front parlor, resting on a broom. Sam lifted his hat politely and his longish hair fell over his ears. "Good mornin', ma'am. I hate to be a bother, but I'm lookin' for one of your roomers. Miss McGee, I believe her name is."

The woman looked at him for several seconds. Then she came to the door and looked at him some more. "You're a queer-lookin' bird," she told him finally. "I ain't seen a rig like that since the buffalo runners was here back in . . ." She started counting on her fingers but soon gave up. "Lordy, I don't know *how* long it's been. Where'd you come from, anyhow?"

Sam drew himself up with dignity. "Madam, my name is California Sam. I am a man of medicine. As I stated earlier, I am callin' this mornin' on a roomer of yours, a Miss Rose McGee."

"You don't look like any doc I ever seen before."

"Not a doctor, madam, a man of medicine. I'd be much obliged if you called Miss McGee for me."

"There wasn't no docs here at all at the time the buffalo runners was here. Shootin' and killin' and skinnin' and peggin'! I never seen the like before or since. Clouds of flies used to swarm around the green hides. Looked like thunderheads."

Sam took a deep breath and said patiently, "Miss McGee, ma'am, if you don't mind."

"I don't mind. She ain't here. What're you doin' in a rig like that, anyhow? You look somethin' like a feller I seen in a wild West show over at Caldwell last year."

Sam made a desperate effort to calm his jangled nerves. "You say Miss McGee ain't here?"

"Pulled out last night, bag and baggage. This feller I was tellin' you about, he pitched glass balls up in the air and shot 'em down with a rifle. It looked like a rifle from where I was sittin'. Somebody said it was a scattergun. You wouldn't be the feller I saw, would you?"

"No ma'am," Sam said resignedly.

"Too bad. I've often wondered if it was really a rifle he was usin'. If it was, I'd like to meet up with him. Don't see many crackshots like that nowadays."

"Miss McGee?"

"Rose?" The woman looked at him with dark, lively eyes. "Rose ain't here. I thought I told you that."

"Do you know where she went?"

"What makes you ask? You're her kinfolks or somethin'?"

"No ma'am," Sam said, wiping his aching forehead, "nothin' like that. I just wanted to talk to her."

"She ain't here. Lit out in the middle of the night, like I already told you. Ever'thing fair and square, though. Paid up every cent she owed before she left."

Sam was beginning to feel dizzy. "Ma'am, have you got any notion where she was headed?"

The woman squinted at him. She had just about made up her mind that he was simple minded at the very least, and probably much worse. "Why, she never said. But I figgered that she went to see her man. She's been talkin' about it for quite a spell now."

"Her man?"

"The one she aimed to marry. You don't know Rose very well if she didn't tell you that."

"No ma'am, I don't know her very well. Where does this man of hers live, could you tell me that?"

"Down in the Cherokee Outlet somewheres. Lookin' for a farm. Lot of foolishness, if you ask me. He's a cowhand, and they make mighty poor farmers."

Sam's stomach was going sour. He found it harder and harder to follow the old woman's rambling thoughts. "How could she leave town in the middle of the night? Did she have a horse or rig?"

"Not that I know about." The woman shrugged. The subject of Rose McGee was clearly beginning to bore her. "She could of rented an outfit at the livery barn, I guess. If she had the money."

She had the money, all right, Sam thought bitterly. He began backing away from the door. "I'm much obliged for your help, ma'am." He settled his hat on his roaring head.

"Do you happen to know," the woman asked, "if it was a rifle that feller in Caldwell was usin'? Or was it a shotgun?"

"I'll see if I can find out," Sam promised with a courtly bow, "and I'll let you know."

At the shed behind the livery barn Sam paused to admire a strange-looking wagon. The running gears of the vehicle were of sturdy Studebaker stock. The body was an awkward boxlike affair, canvas topped, its sides painted with gaudy likenesses of California Sam in a number of heroic poses. The rear of the wagon was outfitted with a let-down platform, similar to a range cook's let-down table on a chuck wagon.

Sam's sagging spirits were lifted momentarily by the colorful artwork on the sides of the wagon—he especially favored a picture of himself in immaculate buckskins effortlessly overcoming an enormous grizzly bear with his bare hands. The gilt words about the picture indicated that the wagon was the property of California Sam, the White Wa-Hoe Medicine Man, the Rage of European Society, Honored Lecturer in the World's Great Institutions of

Learning, not to mention Discoverer of that Medical Sensation of the Ages, Wa-Hoe Indian Herb Mixture.

To think, Sam reflected sadly, that such a man could allow himself to be hoodwinked by a common saloon woman! His uplifted spirits fell with a thud.

He all but gave up the notion of recovering the stickpin. How could a man hope to find one lone woman in that vast ocean of grass known as the Cherokee Outlet? Still, a man had his pride. He had to try. He went into the livery barn and called to the stablehand.

"Bring up my mules, sir," Sam told the stablehand with all the pomposity he could muster. "Hitch them up for me, if you please. To my regret, I find that I must leave Wichita within the hour, on a matter of urgent business." He had learned long ago that when a personage of the stature of California Sam spoke to a "native," the "native" expected to be talked down to.

The stablehand obediently brought up the mules and hitched them to the wagon. A dull-looking man in his middle years, he held out his hand and said, "That'll be two dollars for the board of the animals."

Sam grandly ignored the outstretched hand. "Sir," he said, as if he were addressing a federal judge, "may I inquire whether you were on duty at the rent corral last night?"

The stablehand blinked and reluctantly let his hand drop to his side. "Yes sir. I was cleanin' out the stalls."

"I wonder if Miss Rose McGee who is employed at Omar's Western Trail Saloon, rented a vehicle from you sometime late last night?"

"No sir, she never did."

Sam was puzzled. How could the woman hope to reach the Cherokee Outlet without a rig of some kind, or at least a saddle animal? "You didn't see Miss McGee at all last night?"

"Yes sir," the stablehand said brightly. "I seen her all right. I sold her a horse and saddle." He shuffled his feet and looked slightly guilty about something. "Tell you the truth, it wasn't much of a horse. Or saddle, either. But I let her have it at a good price, I didn't try to cheat her."

"Just to settle my curiosity," Sam said heavily, "would you mind tellin' me what she paid for that horse and saddle?"

"I was askin' fifty dollars, but I settled for forty dollars and a gold-plated watch, seein' that she was a woman and seemed to be in a hurry."

Sam didn't ask to see the watch. He knew whose watch it would be, and he knew that getting his bile stirred up again would only make his head ache. "Bought a horse and saddle," he said dully, "and lit out. In the middle of the night?"

"Yes sir. That's Miss Rose for you. Plenty of spunk."

"Did you happen to notice what direction she headed?"

The stablehand pointed with a grimy finger. "South. Makin' a beeline for the Oklahoma border." Smiling vacantly, he held out his hand and repeated, "That'll be two dollars for the board of the mules."

Two dollars. Rose McGee hadn't even left him a dime for a short glass of beer, but Sam made a pretense of searching his pockets for the money. The stablehand waited with peasantlike patience. He took off his hat and wiped his face with a soiled bandanna, and Sam's flagging spirits took a sudden turn for the better. The man's head was as beautifully bald as a peeled onion.

Sam froze. He stared bug-eyed at the man's head. "Sir," Sam told him with a sorrowful sight, "forgive me for starin'. I know it ain't the thing to do in polite society. However, when a man has devoted his life, as I have, to benefiting mankind and, if I may say so, correctin' the mistakes of Nature . . . well, when I run up against a case like yours . . ."

The stablehand stared at him in amazement. "Case like mine?"

Magically, California Sam no longer felt like a man whose time was running out. He was that rare phenomenon, the natural-born pitchman, forever infatuated with the sound of his own voice. He could no more resist playing to a receptive audience, even a single yokel, than a honeybee could unconcernedly fly past a field of flowering clover. He lowered his voice to a confidential whisper. "Baldness!" he hissed, as if he were speaking of the devil himself. "Obviously," he went on, "you didn't hear my lecture last night when I was speakin' to the gents in front of Omar's Western Trail Saloon."

The stablehand, with a startled expression on his plain face, was shaking his head. "No sir, I never did. I was here, like I told you, cleanin' out the stalls."

"That, as I have already noted," Sam assured him, "is perfectly obvious. If you had heard that lecture, sir, you would be a different man today. A different *man!* Do you know what I mean?"

"No sir," the "native" confessed, "I don't reckon I do."

"Look at my head, sir!" Dramatically, California Sam swept off his broad-brimmed beaver hat and revealed a luxuriant thatch of straw colored hair, a head of hair which, by conservative estimate, had profited the Wa-Hoe Electric Hair Restorer pitch by many hundreds of dollars.

"See that hair!" Sam demanded in rolling tones. "Sir, would you believe that just five years ago there wasn't a single hair on my head. Not a *hair!* Bald as a smooth rock at the bottom of a pool. Oh, don't think I don't know what it's like to be a baldheaded man, sir. The ridicule I've suffered! The sneers of my friends when my back was turned. But worst of all . . ." Again he lowered his voice. "Worst of all," he went on, "is the way the fairer sex, the ladies, look down on a baldheaded man. I tell you, sir, baldheadedness is the curse of our civilization. The broken hearts it has caused! The humiliation! Don't think for a minute that I don't appreciate your misery, sir. For years I too longed in vain for the attentions of a good woman."

"I'm married," the stablehand said.

"Then," Sam plowed on undismayed, "you owe it to that good wife of yours to give her a husband with a full head of hair!" Quickly, he opened his valise and took out a jar of Wa-Hoe Electric Hair Restorer. He stared reverently at the squat, unlovely container. "There you are, sir, the magical salve of the savage Wa-Hoe Indians!"

Despite a throbbing head and uneasy stomach, California Sam was drawn irresistibly into his pitch.

As a young man—so the pitch had it—he had gone hunting for bear in those high, terrible mountains of California where the savage Wa-Hoe Indians made their home. One day he came upon a small Indian boy who had been terribly mauled by a bear. At the risk of his very life Sam took the boy in his arms and, with incredible difficulty, carried him to the main camp of the Wa-Hoes. As it turned out, the youth was none other than San-To, the only son of Ho-Wa-Wa, the great chief of all the Wa-Hoes. There was wild rejoicing in the Indian camp. Instead of torturing and killing Sam, as was the Wa-Hoes' custom with white intruders, he was awarded the highest honors and initiated into the tribe. As a blood brother of the great Ho-Wa-Wa, all the secrets of the Wa-Hoe medicine men were made known to him. Indeed, he became a full-fledged medicine man, licensed, as it were, to practice among the Indians themselves. When at last the time came for him to leave the Indians and return to his own people, the head medicine man of the Wa-Hoes called him aside and revealed to him the last and greatest secret of that great people.

"Bear in mind, sir," Sam told the bug-eyed stablehand, "at the time I'm talkin' about I was as bald as an egg. I couldn't help noticin' that the Wa-Hoes had beautiful black hair, as thick and shiny as a man would ever want to see. Of course I figgered it was a natural thing with the Indians to have beautiful hair. Nothin' could of been farther from the truth. That old medicine man mixed up a batch of electric salve, showin' me just how to do it as he went along. Well sir, then he put a little of that salve on my head and kind of smeared it around. Almost faster than I can tell you about it, I could feel it goin' to work. I could feel it tingle, like the hair was already beginnin' to grow. Sure enough, by the next day I had hair on my head almost an inch long. It grew at the rate of an inch a day until it got about to where it is now. If I wanted more hair than I've got now, why I'd just rub on a little more of this salve. But it happens I'm a man of moderation. Hair, like anything else, can be overdone."

Sam studied the yokel with his hound-dog eyes. He was hooked. "Friend," he said, shaking his head sadly, "I'm sorry you wasn't at that lecture last night. I make a practice never to offer this magical preparation more than once. It's a promise I made to the Wa-Hoes. Indians are different from civilized folks like you and me. They got queer notions about some things. Like opportunity."

The stablehand looked at him dully. He wasn't sure that he knew what opportunity was.

"Whenever Old Man Opportunity steps up and knocks on your door," Sam continued patiently, "why the Wa-Hoes figger they ought to hark and take advantage. Like the gents that listened to my lecture last night. They heard Old Man Opportunity knockin'. They took advantage, and they're happier men this mornin', let me tell you. Walkin' the streets with their backs straight as ramrods, their heads high in the air, *proud!* And why is that, sir? Well, I'll tell you. It's because they got *hair* on their heads. Beautiful, healthy hair, like the Almighty intended for them to have."

"I couldn't hear the lecture," the native objected mildly, "because I was cleanin' out the stalls."

California Sam appeared to be startled by this statement. "That's right! It clean slipped my mind for a minute!" His sagging face brightened. He fairly glowed with affection for his fellow man. "Well, sir, you're a lucky man indeed! I'm goin' to break a lifelong habit—and I'm tellin' you right now, if the Wa-Hoes ever found out about it I'd be in bad trouble—I'm goin' to give you a second chance, sir. A second *chance*. I'm goin' to break a promise that I made to old Chief Ho-Wa-Wa hisself. I'm goin' to let Opportunity knock a second time." He shot anxious glances all around to make sure that some lurking Wa-Hoe wasn't watching. With the air of a crooked gambler palming an ace of spades, he quickly pressed the small jar of Electric Hair Restorer into the sucker's hand.

That was that. Once a yokel had the merchandise in his hand it was as good as sold. "No, no! I don't want any pay!" Sam said sharply, as if the stablehand had been pressing money on him at the point of a gun. "Breakin' my promise to old Ho-Wa-Wa is bad enough—acceptin' money would be temptin' fate too much!"

He climbed up on the wheel of the wagon and took his place on the driver's seat. "The board of my animals is all the pay I can take," he told the dumfounded stablehand. "Please don't ask me to accept anything more." With a dignified nod of his head he released the brake and drove out of the wagon yard.

In a way, Sam thought as he headed the wagon away from the huge maze of shipping pens, it was a shame that he had to be leaving Wichita so soon. With enough suckers like the stablehand, he would soon have been a rich man. He might even make up for the loss of the diamond stickpin.

On the other hand, of course, Wichita abounded in light-fingered saloon women like Rose McGee. So maybe it was just as well to look for a new place.

By midday California Sam was well away from Wichita, and not a minute too soon. When a medicine man dealt in "electric goods" such as the Hair Restorer, he had to be ready to pull stakes at a moment's notice. The capsicum ointment that caused the native's scalp to tingle and convinced him that hair was actually beginning to grow also had a dangerous tendency to turn the yokel's head beet-red. Within a few days his scalp would begin to peel and flake like cheap paint on a barn wall. The wise medicine man saved his hair restorer pitch for his last day in town, or, if possible, the last hour.

But all that was ancient history now. A pitchman's life was filled with dangerous situations—a miscalculation of yokel psychology had meant disaster to many a medicine man—but for the moment Sam was reasonably content. He forced his thoughts away from Rose McGee and the lost stickpin. New adventures lay beyond the shaggy horizon. New suckers to fleece. Taken all in all, he philosophized, life was not too unpleasant. As long as a man kept his health.

2

WHEN Dutch Rainey got out of bed that morning he went directly to the washstand mirror and inspected his head for new growth. His scalp was a lively, glowing pink. He winced as he touched it with his fingertip. The medicine show doc had said there would be a tingling sensation, which meant that new hair was beginning to force its way through the scalp. But tingling wasn't the word for it. "Burning," and a fierce "itching," came closer to describing the sensation that Dutch Rainey was feeling.

For a long while he studied his reflection in disbelief. Little by little his first reactions of shock and anger passed away. A quivering rage took its place. The longer he looked at himself the more violent it became. Suddenly he wheeled from the washstand and gave his partner's bunk a savage kick. "Get up!"

Billy Prince, who had been snoring loudly on the top bunk, rolled over and stared in fascination at his pal's head.

Dutch's mouth was pulled down savagely. His pale eyes glittered. Between muttered curses he pulled on his pants and stamped into his boots. "Get up!" he said again with a snarl.

"Where we goin'?" Billy asked cautiously.

"Back to town and find a medicine show doc."

Billy sat on the edge of his bunk in his union suit. The air in the small line shack fairly crackled with Dutch's anger. "What," he asked carefully, "do you want with a medicine show doc?"

"I ain't decided yet. Maybe I'll kill him."

"Not in Wichita," Billy said with the cool logic of a man whose scalp was not on fire. "Unless you're anxious to get yourself hung."

Dutch Rainey glared at his partner. "Maybe I'll just hold him down and make him eat a few jars of this hair restorin' salve and see how he likes it. I told you, I ain't decided yet." He returned to the washstand and dribbled cool water over his burning head. But the relief was only temporary, and the return of the fiery itching only aggravated his rage.

Billy Prince eyed his partner thoughtfully but did not move from his place on the bunk. Except for his unpredictable temper, Dutch Rainey was a good enough man to ride with. He and Billy had been together almost two years. They had known good times and hard times, but taken all together it had been a satisfactory partnership. Until now.

Billy didn't like that broken glass glitter in Dutch's eyes. There was no doubt in Billy's mind that Dutch would cheerfully have murdered that medicine show doc, if he could have laid hands on him at that moment. Given a few hours, or a few days, maybe Dutch's temper would cool and he'd be willing to settle for something less than blood. On the other hand, maybe he wouldn't. Billy decided he'd rather not take the chance.

"It's a mistake," he told his partner quietly, "goin' lookin' for that doc, the shape your temper's in."

Dutch glared at him. "Are you goin' to get your clothes on or ain't you?"

Billy shook his head. "We got a good thing here; I ain't ready to let it go. Up to now the law ain't got anything against us, unless you want to count robbin' the stagecoach down in the Territory. It would be a fool thing to do, linin' ourselves up for a hangin', just because you got a blistered head."

"You don't want to ride along," Dutch snarled at him, "that's all right with me."

Billy shrugged his shoulders and sighed. "I guess that's the way it'll have to be."

Dutch's face became almost as red as his scalp. He slammed out of the line shack and began throwing a saddle on a company horse. Against his better judgment, Billy dropped down from the bunk and called to his partner from the doorway. "It ain't goin' to help things if you ride off on one of the boss' horses. If they don't hang you for murder, they'll get you for horse stealin'."

Dutch told him in several well-chosen obscenities what the boss could do about the horse. Billy sighed again and shrugged his shoulders in resignation. "Well," he said, "if you change your mind, leave the animal at the wagon yard in Wichita. I'll tell the boss where to find it."

Billy watched with flagging interest as Dutch rode away from the half-dugout line shack. Well, he thought philosophically, it had been an interesting two years that he and Dutch had ridden together. A bank robbed in Missouri. The stagecoach in the Cherokee Nation. A spell of rustling in Texas. But lately they had been living a restful life here in line camp, quietly tending the boss' cattle, well away from the curious eyes of county sheriffs and federal marshals. Of course, things never remained restful for long when you parded with Dutch Rainey. Every so often he would have to slip off to see the elephant, as he called it, in Wichita. "I might of known," Billy told himself, "that sooner or later he'd run into a sharpshooter like that medicine show doc, and there'd be hell to pay."

Billy Prince had the uneasy feeling that his own restful days were coming to an end. He raised a hand and half-heartedly saluted the distant figure of Dutch Rainey. "So long, Dutch, and good luck. You're goin' to need it."

But it wasn't really Dutch that he felt concern for. It was the medicine show pitchman who needed all the luck.

Dutch Rainey rode with his hat on his saddle horn and a blue bandanna wrapped around his blistered head. Every few minutes he would moisten the bandanna with a little water from his canteen. It briefly relieved the agony of itching, but nothing could relieve the rage in his brain. As he rode he devised exotic ways of murdering the pitchman. Maybe he would shave his head and smear it all over with Electric Hair Restorer and watch him suffer for a day or two before shooting him. Maybe he would put a funnel in his mouth and pour his own Wa-Hoe Indian Herb Mixture down his gullet until he exploded like a dead toad in the sun.

It was midafternoon when Dutch raised the dusty cowtown of Wichita. It was not the town it had once been, when cattle from all of Texas had been funneled into her shipping pens. No more riding hell for leather into town and shooting off your pistol just because you felt like it. No more fancy dance hall girls hollering at you from second-story windows. Law and order and respectability were the order of the day, and Wichita—as far as Dutch Rainey was concerned—was the worse town for it.

But at that moment Dutch was not thinking about days that had long since passed into history. He tied up in front of Omar's Western Trail Saloon and tramped inside.

The barkeep took one look at Dutch's bandanna-wrapped head and heaved a sigh of exasperation. He held up a hand, stopping Dutch before he could open his mouth.

"Lissen to me, mister. The medicine show doc ain't here. He was here this mornin' early, but he ain't here any more. That's all I know."

Dutch pulled up short, squinting angrily. "How'd you know I was lookin' for the medicine man?"

"You're the fourth one that's been in here today. All of you with your heads wrapped up in pieces of wet cloth, all of you threatenin' to kill the medicine man when you find him. Well, that's all right with me. But first you'll have to find him. He ain't here."

"He was here last night, with one of your saloon women. I seen them myself."

With an air of a man whose patience has been tried almost beyond endurance, the barkeep nodded. "Rose McGee. But that was last night. She ain't here either, and I don't know where she is."

A customer at the lower end of the bar gestured for service. The barkeep started to move away when Dutch lunged forward, reached across the bar and grabbed the man by the throat. "Don't get fancy with me!" he snarled in the barkeep's startled face. "A buckskin dude like that medicine man don't just go up like Apache smoke—he's got to be somewheres. And I figger you know where."

"Mister," the barkeep said nervously, "I'm tellin' you the truth. He was in here first thing this mornin', mean as a snake hisself, lookin' for Rose. Where he went from here I don't know. Wait a minute," he added, getting an idea. "There was a kid that did some work for him. Maybe he could tell you where he went."

"What kid?" Dutch snarled without letting go of the barkeep's throat.

"Jones his name is. Just a stray that wandered into Wichita a few weeks ago."

"Where does he stay?"

"He does cleanin' jobs at the wagon yard. You could try there."

"If you're dancin' me around," Dutch told him coldly, "I'll come back and set fire to this business of yours."

His next stop was the wagon yard. The hostler gazed idly at Dutch's blue-bandaged head and said, "You're the fourth one today to come askin' for that medicine show doc. He ain't here. If I knew where he was I'd tell you. I might even help you shoot him; my stablehand's gone home with a blistered head hisself, leavin' me with all the stalls to clean. The kid ain't here either. He was here this mornin'; that's the last I seen of him. Maybe him and the doc went off together."

Dutch began to realize that settling scores with California Sam was apt to take more time than he had first planned on. With admirable self-control, he curbed his flaring temper and demanded, "Which way did the doc head when he left the wagon yard?"

The hostler pointed generally to the south. "The stablehand said he was makin' for Oklahoma country. He won't be easy to find on the prairie."

"I'll find him," Dutch vowed. "Don't you fret about that."

Shortly before sundown California Sam prepared to make camp on one of the lesser forks of the Arkansas. He was reasonably pleased with the progress he had made since leaving Wichita. He had skillfully mingled his tracks with the tracks of countless other travelers headed for the new lands of Oklahoma. There was no sign of angry yokels with glowing pink scalps bearing down on him from the north.

"Boys," he said to the world at large, "forgettin' the loss of my diamond stickpin for the moment, as well as a certain thievin'-hearted, redheaded saloon woman I could mention, you got to admit that things could be a sight worse." He reached into the wagon for his store of grain alcohol. He dragged out a five-gallon coal oil can, poured a little of the clear liquid into a tin cup and downed it.

As drinking liquor it was nothing to be especially proud

of—on the other hand, it beat no liquor at all by a considerable margin. Alcohol, to a medicine man, was what tobacco was to a cigar manufacturer. Without plenty of the fiery liquid to mix with his herbs, there would be no Wa-Hoe Indian Herb Mixture.

He poured himself another small dram, then unhitched the mules and put them out to graze. He let down the rear platform and rummaged in the wagon until he located a side of slightly rancid bacon and a can of tomatoes. Then, to his amazement, an odd-shaped bulge began to stir in the corner of the wagon. The figure rose up ghostlike, beneath a waterproof sheet and said, "I knew it all the time! You never aimed to pay me my dollar!"

California Sam stared dumfounded at two small, angry eyes that glared at him from beneath the wagon sheet. "Hell and damnation!" he finally exploded. "What're you doin' in my wagon, boy?"

"You told me I could come with you," the boy said sullenly.

"When did I say a thing like that?"

"Yesterday. The same time you told me you'd pay me my dollar." Hassle Jones threw off the piece of tarp that he had been hiding under. "And you drove off and beat the hotel out of *their* money, too. I *told* you that's what you aimed to do."

"Get out of my wagon!" Sam hollered at him. "What the hell, you loco or somethin'?"

"I just did what you told me I could do."

"I never said nothin' of the kind! Get out of there!" He reached in and hauled the hostile boy down to the ground. "All right now," Sam said, puffing up indignantly. "What's got into you, anyhow? What do you mean leavin' home that way, without as much as a 'goodgo to hell' to your family?"

"I ain't got a home," young Hassle Jones told him boldly.

"Don't get fancy with me, boy. Everybody's got a home."

"Well . . ." The boy shrugged. "I been sleepin' in the loft at the wagon yard, if that's what you mean."

Sam squinted at him, his temper cooling. "That's all the home you had?"

"It was all right. I don't complain."

"Then why did you sneak in my wagon and run off?"

"I want to see the elephant," the boy told him coolly. "Wichita's a tame town. Nothin' ever happens there."

Somethin' would of happened today, Sam thought to himself, if I'd took much longer gettin' out. To the boy, he said sourly, "Well, I guess I can't start you walkin' back across the prairie to Wichita on an empty stomach." He flapped his arms resignedly. "So make yourself handy. Rustle up some firewood."

Sam stirred up a batch of hoecake and cooked it in hot bacon fat. Hunkered down beside the fire, they wolfed the bread and bacon. They speared tomatoes out of the can and then drank the juice. "You drink coffee?" Sam asked the youth.

"Everybody drinks coffee."

They found an extra tin cup in the chuck box and sat drinking the thick, bitter coffee. Darkness came down on the Kansas prairie. They could hear wild turkeys settling down to roost in the cottonwoods along the creek. Sam brought out a corncob pipe, filled it with black, coarse tobacco and lit it. The night was warm and soft, and the smell of tobacco gave it spice.

At last Sam said, "What about your ma?"

"Dead," Hassle Jones told him. "That was long time ago. I don't recollect much about her."

"How about your pa?"

"Horse fell on him when I was six years old. He lingered that summer, but his ribs punctured his lungs. He died."

"Where you been livin' all this time? Besides the wagon yard."

Hassle was silent for several seconds. He flipped some

gravel into the fire and shot quick, sidelong glances at Sam from beneath his shaggy hair. "Part of the time with kinfolks," he said at last.

"What kinfolks?"

"My uncle's bunch. My ma's brother. He farms a little place over in Missouri."

"That's a long way from Wichita. How come you to leave?"

"I'm fiddlefooted," the boy told him dryly. "I like to travel."

Sam snorted, tamped his pipe and relit. He didn't believe a word of the kid's story. As a pitchman, he considered it a point of professional honor never to believe *any*body's story. Not that he cared one way or another. The next day, or the day after that, they would come to a town and he would send the kid packing. In the meantime the two of them would have to make the best of each other's company.

"I don't guess you thought to bring a bed, did you," Sam asked, "when you decided to stow away in my wagon?"

Hassle Jones shrugged his thin shoulders. "I don't need a bed. I can sleep anywhere."

With poor grace, Sam found an extra blanket and a piece of tarp in the wagon and gave them to him. "Right now," he said, "we better come to an understandin' about some things. First off, I'm a high pitchman. And I'm a single. Nobody ever travels with me—not even to ballyhoo the crowds. I do my own ballyhoo. So I never told you that you could come with me, even if I was drunk at the time. Have we got that much straight?"

The boy shrugged but did not look intimidated. "I guess. What's a high pitchman?"

"A high pitchman," Sam told him with considerable pride, "does his ballyhoo and lectures from a platform. A low pitchman makes his pitch from a tripod or table, on the same level with the suckers. High pitchmen are the chiefs, low pitchmen are the Indians."

"How'd you get to be a medicine show man?" Hassle asked.

"How does a preacher get to be a preacher? He does what he's cut out to do. He feels it here . . ." Sam thumped his chest in the vicinity of his heart. "He feels that he's cut out to be somethin' special, somethin' above the common run of mankind. Well, I heard the call when I was a young man. I decided to be a pitchman."

"You never wanted to be anything better?"

California Sam looked appalled. "Boy, are you serious? What on the good Lord's beautiful green earth could be better than bein' a high pitchman?"

"I don't know," the boy said. "But you pulled out of Wichita just two jumps ahead of a horsewhippin'. Is that what it's like to be a pitchman?"

Sam sighed to himself, hauled out the coal oil can and poured himself a stiff shot of clear alcohol. "You ain't nothin' but a child, boy. There ain't no way I could tell you what it's like being a first-class pitchman."

"You could try," Hassle said. "I ain't sleepy yet."

To Sam's surprise, he was finding that having some company on the road was mildly pleasant, even if it was only a kid. He lounged back against the wagon wheel and refilled his pipe. "All right, get the cookin' things good and clean. Then move the mules deeper into the bottom where the grass is better. When you're all finished I'll tell you about Fifth Street and Main, in Los Angeles, California."

Hassle quickly rinsed the skillet and tin plates and rubbed them shiny with sand. He moved the mules to where the grass was lushest and then came back and settled expectantly by the fire.

"Do you know," Sam asked, "where Los Angeles, California is?"

"I ain't sure," Hassle frowned. "Across the mountains somewhere, ain't it?"

"That's right. Just as far west as you can go. And when

you're smack up against the beautiful Pacific Ocean, there's the city. A real hustle-bustle, step-lively city, boy. A thousand times bigger'n Wichita, a thousand times noisier and more excitin'. And right there in the middle of it all is Fifth Street and Main. There's a big house where medicine men gather in the winter, if they can, to rest their bodies and spirits in the warm California sun. Some of the medicine men live in the house, but most of them just pitch there and live somewheres else. They pitch from the front porch at all hours of the day and night. The yokels gang around in the front yard, eatin' oranges out of paper sacks, just itchin' to be fleeced! I tell you, boy, it comes mighty close to bein' paradise here on earth!"

Hassle asked, "Was you ever there yourself, in Los Angeles, California?"

"Sure I was," Sam told him proudly. "Many a time. Why there was one winter I won't never forget. Big excursion trains was haulin' fresh yokels in from the sticks every day. They practically forced us to take their money. Before two months was out I had five thousand dollars in my pocket, and two real diamond rings on my fingers." He thought about those days for a moment with a lax, bittersweet expression on his long face. "If it hadn't been for slow horses and fast women . . ."

"Women like Miss Rose McGee at the Western Trail Saloon?"

The memory of that brief encounter caused California Sam to squirm. "Boy," he said ruefully, "every man is born to a certain set of strengths and weaknesses. I'm afraid my big weakness is women."

"What other places have you seen? Besides Los Angeles, California?"

"Just about every place, boy. From the hop houses in St. Mary's Alley in San Francisco, to the dark, shufflin' streets of New Orleans, Louisiana. I even went to Vancouver once. Took a steamboat all the way to Canada. It was a fine, pretty place to look at, but the yokels didn't have much money." He heaved a sigh. "A medicine man goes everywhere. I guess it's in the blood."

Sam brought out the coal oil can and poured himself another drink. "What about the Wa-Hoe Indians?" Hassle asked.

"The Wa-Hoes? Heaven help you, boy, there ain't any Wa-Hoe Indians. Except in the brain of a San Francisco newspaperman that I paid to write that lecture for me. Don't tell me you believed that yarn about me savin' the son of that old Indian chief!"

"You're the first medicine show man I ever heard."

"Well, I'll give you some free advice—during your lifetime it'll save you thousands of dollars, if you heed it. Never believe anything a woman tells you, or anything you hear from a lecture platform."

California Sam made his bed inside the wagon, as he always did when he was on the road. Young Hassle Jones slept beneath the wagon on his borrowed bedding. When morning came Sam roused himself reluctantly and peered out at the damp, prairie summer dawn. He was surprised to see a lively blaze going in the fire trench. There was a brisk, heady aroma of coffee in the air.

Hassle Jones was struggling up from the creek bottom lugging a bucket of fresh water. "I been seein' to the mules," the boy told California Sam. "Gave them a little mess of shelled corn that I found in a sack under the driver's seat. Was that all right?"

Sam blinked his bloodshot eyes several times. Coffee had already been put on to boil. The skillet was on the fire; the meat was cooking. It was a little unnerving to wake up and discover everything so well in hand so early in the morning. Early morning, as the general rule, was not California Sam's best part of the day.

"Boy," he said sourly, "what the hell you think you're doin'?"

"Gettin' breakfast," Hassle told him mildly. "I would of stirred up some flapjacks, but I couldn't find the wheat flour."

"There ain't any wheat flour," Sam grumbled, climbing out of the wagon. "What does a boy your age know about gettin' breakfast anyhow?"

Hassle set the bucket down and said in an odd tone, "It's somethin' I learned when I was stayin' with my uncle's bunch."

Sam dipped into the bucket of water and washed his face and hands. He poured himself some of the coffee–it was black and strong and not too gritty, which was all a reasonable man could ask of trail coffee. The bacon was suitably thick and had not been overcooked. The tainted edges had been trimmed away. "Just like the Windsor Hotel in Denver," Sam said dryly and stamped away to look at the mules.

The truth was that California Sam was not used to having his work done for him. He was not sure that he liked it. Contrary to popular thought, Sam had learned that it usually paid to look gift horses very closely in the mouth.

"Hold on a minute," he said, as Hassle began heating water for dish washing. He filled his first pipe of the day and lit it with a sulphur match. "It's been my experience," he said ponderously, "that when a body starts to make hisself right handy for no good reason, he's up to somethin'. He's in trouble. Or he wants somethin'. Which one is it with you?"

The boy looked at him indignantly. "I ain't in any trouble. And the only thing I want is a ride to the Oklahoma country."

"Why didn't you come to me and ask straight-out for a ride?"

"Would you of let me come?"

Sam shrugged and had to admit, "I guess not."

"That's why I didn't ask."

The youth's logic was difficult to deny. "When you get done with the dishes," Sam growled at him, "you can bring up the mules and get them hitched."

Sometime that afternoon they left Kansas behind them and entered the great stretch of grassland that went by the name of Cherokee Outlet. This was new country; it had been settled for less than a year. Making headway in a wagon was a slow business over roads that were all but non-existent.

Every hour or so Hassle would stand on the driver's seat and stare out at the ocean of grass. "You sure this is Oklahoma. It looks pretty much the same as Kansas to me."

"It's Oklahoma, all right," Sam told him. "If you want to believe this government map." From time to time he would stop the team and consult one of the large folding maps that were sold to prospective land seekers. Dead ahead, according to a nervous line on the drawing, was supposed to be the Little Arkansas. Somewhere in the neighborhood was the railroad town of Pond Creek. This was Sam's immediate destination. Railroads meant business, money, and a reliable flow of suckers making for the promised land of Oklahoma. The thought of Pond Creek caused California Sam to relax somewhat and smile to himself. In such a place a man of daring and imagination might very well build a respectable bankroll for himself.

From time to time they would catch a glimpse of a settler's sod house standing forlornly on the prairie. Standing there, Sam thought, like a wart on the face of an unlovely woman. They saw a man breaking his back and killing his mules trying to break the tough prairie sod. Once a stair-step passel of children scurried out and waved excitedly to the man and boy in the gaudily painted wagon.

"Sodbusters," California Sam said superiorly. "Nothin' here for a medicine man. Got to catch them at the depot when they get off the train. Before some crooked real estate man fleeces them." In a new country like this, medicine men and real estate men were natural enemies, and their natural prey was the green settler who had the wide-eyed notion that a new country meant a new start, new hope.

Hassle Jones, who had learned something about farming in Missouri, looked pained at the sight of a scrawny mule struggling to pull a turning plow through that thick sod. "How are they ever goin' to get anything to grow in *that* kind of ground?"

"They ain't, boy," Sam told him loftily. "This here's grassland, as any fool can see. But no use tryin' to tell that to a yokel. If it's a piece of ground, a sucker'll try to grow somethin' on it. I guess it's in his blood." He heaved a huge sigh and shook his head. "I got to admit, boy, that there are times when I'm tempted to give up medicine and go into real estate."

The day passed quietly. Sam allowed the mules to travel at their own pace, and occasionally he would nip from the five gallon coal oil can beneath the driver's seat. And he talked. Talking came as naturally as breathing to California Sam, and in young Hassle Jones he had an attentive and appreciative audience.

"There was a time down in Louisiana once, when I was ballyhoolin' for a Quaker doc. He was a high pitchman with good flash, a specialist in chopped grass and corn slum. Well, one day this native come up to the platform where the doc was lecturin' . . ."

The population of the earth, according to California Sam, was divided neatly into two parts. On one side stood the pitchmen; on the other side was everybody else. A customer was never simply a customer; he was a yokel, a chump, a sucker, a native. The pitchman's language, to the ears of young Hassle Jones, was delightfully colorful. There were high pitchmen and low pitchmen, as he had already heard. A trick or gimmick to attract the yokel to the platform was called a "punch." The medicine man's rapid-fire monologue that he kept going while selling his wares was called the "grind." A "moll buzzer" was a purse snatcher.

A "clockman" was a thief who specialized in watches. Any kind of stage atmosphere or backdrop was called a "flash." "Ballyhoo," was any kind of pre-pitch act to attract the chumps to the platform. Liquid medicine of any kind was "slum." "Corn slum" was a liquid that supposedly removed corns from the natives' aching toes. All herbs were called "chopped grass." Powdered herbs was "flea powder." California Sam even had a special name for Rose McGee—he called her a "pennyweighter." A "pennyweighter," as Hassle soon learned, was a diamond thief.

Medicine men, as Sam explained, were divided generally into three types: the Quaker, the Oriental, and the Indian Scout. In some parts of the country the "Quaker" was most popular. He spoke in "thees" and "thous" and wore black suits and widebrim hats. Quakers were generally accepted as honest, God-fearing men fairly dripping with the milk of human kindness. Rare was the yokel who had the grit to step up to a medicine man in a Quaker suit and tell him to his face that he was a crook. California Sam scratched himself and grinned at the thought of such an unlikely occurrence. "The truth is, boy, I once considered the Quaker pitch myself. But I ain't the type. The Quaker has to keep watch all the time. The chumps see him havin' a quiet drink in a saloon or passin' the time of day with a dance hall woman, and he's finished."

The Oriental medicine man—Sam explained, to continue Hassle's education—was a pitchman of a different stripe. The Oriental and the Indian Scout had much in common. "The Oriental pitch," said Sam, in the round tones of the professional lecturer, "goes somethin' like this."

Many years ago—so the pitch had it—there was a young missionary couple working the Lord's vineyard in the land of the heathen Chinese. It was a time of great troubles. A time of wars and famine. One day a group of savage bandits swooped down on the small settlement where the young missionaries (with their small son) did their good work. The missionaries were brutally slain in the attack. The young boy's life was miraculously spared. (Which miracle, Sam explained, could be as simple or as elaborate as the pitchman wished to make it.) After due suffering and long wandering, the boy found shelter with an old Chinese scholar who was traveling from Lanchow to Lhasa. (Get your details right. You could never be sure there wouldn't be an educated yokel in the crowd.) Finally they came to the old scholar's home in the high, lonesome mountains of southern China. (More detail.) There the boy lived as the old man's own son. Every day the old scholar would read to the boy from manuscripts and books, teaching him the almost-forgotten secrets of an ancient and wise people. As it turned out, the old man was a famous doctor among his own people, and he taught the boy the art of healing, just as the old man's father had taught it to him. In due time the boy became a skilled physician. The simple mountain folk accepted him as almost the equal of the old scholar himself. But as time passed, the boy (now a young man, of course) became restless and longed to return to his own people. Heavy of heart, the old man gave him his blessing and told him yes, it was time now for him to return to the world that his parents had lived in. So, with great sadness, the young man left the mountain village of China, his head full of miraculous secrets of ancient Chinese physicians.

"And the most miraculous secret of all," California Sam intoned, winding up the pitch, "is this secret blend of purified yak butter and the oil of that tiny mountain shrub, considered holy by the Chinese, the tow-tow bush . . ." Sam shot Hassle a sidelong look. "What do you think of it so far?"

"It sounds like the white hunter and the Wa-Hoe medicine man, except in China."

Sam laughed. "Boy, you're one hundred percent right. She's the same pitch right down the line, moved over to a different country and salted with a little imagination, as the pitchman sees fit. But the suckers never catch on. You right sure there wasn't a pitchman in your family somewheres?"

"Not that I ever heard about."

"Well," Sam admitted, "in some families it ain't a thing they talk about."

By the end of the second day they had worked out a practical division of trail chores. Sam drove the team, and Hassle made camp, broke camp, did the cooking, looked after the mules, hitched and unhitched, and washed the dishes.

When Sam wasn't too busy smoking or thinking he would generously spin a few yarns about his own adventures. "Missionary amongst the natives," he called it. Hassle listened open-mouthed as California Sam explained how to "fix" a town, by which he meant the art of finding just the right politician and bribing him with just the right amount of cash in order to obtain a license to sell medicine on a particular corner.

"Location, boy, that's the important thing. The best pitch in the world won't make you a dime if you set up in the boondocks. Find your go-between, pay him whatever he wants, and get yourself a good corner. In San Francisco I once paid a common harness bull fifty dollars a day for the corner at Fifth and Market, and it was cheap at the price."

The education of young Hassle Jones proceeded at a dizzying pace. He learned about the highly profitable catarrh pitch, the razor-strop pitch, the "look-back" pitch. He became acquainted with the low pitch "gummy-ga-ho" men who specialized in hawking glue, with "painless dentists," with shills and pills and opium smokers and drunkards.

"Oh, there's bad ones on the road, like anywhere else," Sam admitted. But he smiled as he said it. In the world of the pitchman every man belonged to the same family. The kinsmen looked after their own—even the black sheep.

3

AFTER forty-eight hours Dutch Rainey's scalp began to shrivel and crack like a mud flat in the July sun. He clawed at it until his fingers were bloody. He cursed the medicine show pitchman until he was hoarse. For the best part of two days and two nights he allowed rage to overwhelm him. He didn't eat and he didn't sleep and he didn't think of anything but finding the pitchman.

Then, late on the second day, he met the drummer.

The drummer's name was Horace Green and his line was shoes. He had come from Caldwell and was making for the new Oklahoma Territory, stopping occasionally at country stores along the way. At the time he first saw Dutch Rainey, Mr. Green was camped on the bank of the Salt Fork of the Arkansas. In the act of cooking supper, Mr. Green looked up and was somewhat alarmed to see the horsebacker bearing down on him from the north.

"Howdy," the drummer said nervously as Dutch reined

his horse down at the edge of the fire. "Get down and have some supper."

The horsebacker answered with a growl in his throat. "I'm lookin' for a medicine show doc that goes by the name of California Sam. Fancy painted wagon, team of gray mules."

"As a matter of fact," said Mr. Green, "I saw such a wagon yesterday. Headed southwest, as I recollect." He tried not to stare at the bloody bandanna on the stranger's head. "There's plenty of food here. You're welcome to share it . . ."

"I ain't hungry," the horsebacker said impatiently. "Yesterday, you say? What time yesterday?"

The shoe drummer thought for a moment. "Why, maybe an hour or so before sundown."

Unexpectedly, the stranger grinned. His lips curled back, baring his teeth. There was something in the expression that chilled the drummer's blood. He asked worriedly, "Is . . . is there somethin' wrong?"

"Nothin' wrong," Dutch Rainey told him through gleaming yellow teeth. "Everything's fine. Much oblige for your help."

He reined his animal away from the fire and headed southwest. A strange and rather frightening man, Mr. Horace Green decided. For a few moments he wondered if he had done the right thing in mentioning that he had seen the medicine man's wagon.

Southwest, the drummer had said. Dutch thought about that. Traveling southwest from Wichita, the medicine man would eventually strike the Rock Island tracks. Dutch reasoned that his man hadn't selected that particular direction by accident, that he was making for one of the new railroad towns in the newly opened Cherokee Outlet. That greatly simplified his search. He would simply head for Pond Creek, the first Rock Island station south of the Kansas line. If California Sam wasn't in Pond Creek, Dutch would simply follow the tracks south until he found him.

For the first time in two days Dutch Rainey became aware of his own exhaustion and the exhaustion of his horse. "Son," he said patting the animal's neck, "pretty soon we'll stop and rest a spell. Now that I know what direction he's headed, we'll catch him. Sooner or later we'll catch him. We'll learn that medicine man that he can't play free and loose with Dutch Rainey!"

That night he made camp beside a clearwater stream and staked the exhausted animal in the lush grass near the water. He built a fire and boiled some coffee and chewed on his emergency ration of jerky. But the coffee was as bitter as buffalo gall. The jerky was tough and stringy; the longer he chewed it the drier it seemed to get, and at last he spit it out in disgust.

What he needed, he told himself, was sleep, so he threw his blanket beneath an umbrella of rattling cottonwoods. But sleep would not come. As soon as he closed his eyes the homely, smirking face of the medicine show pitchman loomed in his mind. His tortured scalp began to itch unbearably. In a fit of rage he threw off the blanket and stamped out the fire and brought the stumbling horse up from the bottom.

It was then that Dutch Rainey knew that he would never be able to rest properly until that devil of a pitchman was laid out for burying.

On their third day out of Wichita, California Sam and Hassle Jones raised their first town in the new territory. "Well, now," Sam beamed, eying the cluster of farm wagons in the dusty street, "we're in luck, boy. It must be Saturday."

Hassle gazed without enthusiasm at the dozen, sorry, unpainted frame shacks that went under the name of Plateau, Oklahoma Territory. The prospect of twenty rickety farm wagons and maybe a hundred sodbusters making their weekly pilgrimage to town did not excite him. But to a pitchman of California Sam's experience, prying a sodbuster loose from his money presented a challenge that he could not resist.

When they neared the outskirts of town Sam pulled the wagon into a wild plum thicket, well out of sight of townsmen and visiting sodbusters. "Look in the equipment box," he told the youth briskly. "There ought to be a wagon jack in there somewheres."

Hassle frowned. "What do you want with a wagon jack?"

"Don't ask fool questions, boy. Do like I tell you."

Obediently, Hassle climbed down, looked in the equipment box and hauled out jack and wheel wrenches. "Now look alive, boy," Sam told him, "and take off that nigh front wheel. We ain't got a lot of time to waste; pretty soon the suckers'll be startin' home to do the evenin's milkin'."

Young Hassle Jones, at the age of eleven, going on twelve, was no stranger to hard work, but he did resent working up a sweat on a hot July afternoon taking off wagon wheels that were obviously in good working order. "I don't see why you want that wheel took off," he said with a hint of a whine.

California Sam, from the comfort of the driver's seat, looked down at him sternly. "Boy, I already told you, don't waste time askin' fool questions."

With considerable difficulty, and a great deal of ill-humored grumbling, Hassle set about getting the jack beneath the axle and raising the wheel off the ground. Up on the driver's seat, Sam was hauling odd-shaped parcels and packages and boxes out of the interior of the wagon. He whistled a lively little tune as he "worked." Clearly, California Sam was happy with the prospect before them. "There ain't nothin'," he said to the sweating youth, "that perks up an old pitchman's spirits like the sight of a hundred yokels all together in one place."

"I got the wheel off," Hassle panted after a long struggle with the wrenches. "What do you want to do now?"

"Clean her up," Sam told him cheerfully. "Here." He handed the boy some coal oil in a glass jar, and some clean rags. "Clean the axle and the hub and the nuts. When you're through I want to see them sparkle."

Hassle shook his head. He was beginning to doubt the pitchman's sanity. But in the end he went to work, cleaning the black, gritty axle grease off the axle and hub and all the locking washers and nuts. While Hassle was doing that, Sam was busily working white laundry soap into a wet sponge. When he was satisfied that the sponge was thoroughly filled with soap he set it on the canvas top of the wagon to dry.

For almost an hour Hassle grumbled and sweated over his cleaning job. In the meantime Sam's soap-filled sponge had dried nicely and he put it with a tray of other items. "It's the women," California Sam explained to the boy who, by that time, was too exhausted to be curious. "When it comes to medicine, women have got suspicious minds. They got a dangerous habit of readin' labels and askin' questions about what they're buyin'. Anyhow, most of them would rather do their doctorin' with coal oil and turpentine and spend their money on dress goods and Hoyt's Cologne. No sir, the medicine pitch ain't for women. It's the menfolks that do the heavy work and get down in their backs and have sour stomachs and bald heads . . ."

California Sam, the platform lecturer, threw his arms wide in an all-knowing gesture. "Anyhow, when there's ladies in the crowd, the pitch has to be changed to suit them. And what is it exactly that the ladies want, my boy? They want somethin' to make work a little easier and life more pleasant. And that's just what we aim to give them. You watch, boy, them farm wives will be shovin' their husbands up to buy this Wa-Hoe Miracle Soap like it was the last ticket on the Ark and the tide was goin' out."

"What Wa-Hoe Miracle Soap?" Hassle asked, taking time out to get his breath.

"This right here," Sam said proudly, holding up a small, shiny object in one hand. For some time the pitchman had been busily cutting large bars of white soap into small pieces, wrapping them in little squares of tinfoil and sticking on labels. "How's that cleanin' job comin'?"

"If you don't think it would strain you too much," the boy told him coolly, "you could get down and see for yourself."

"I'm proud to take your word for it," California Sam told him with a generous wave of his hand. "You say she's clean, she's clean."

"Then she's clean," Hassle told him.

The pitchman beamed down at him, ignoring his surly tone. "Boy, you're goin' to get an education today, absolutely free of charge, that a thousand dollars couldn't buy for you in the finest university in the land. So pay attention. Don't get uppity." He handed the boy something in a gallon syrup bucket. "Here, fill the hub cap with this and smear it good and heavy all around the axle."

Hassle stared at the black, gummy stuff in the bucket. It looked like axle grease, but it didn't smell or feel like axle grease. "What is it?"

"Heaven help you, boy," California Sam chuckled, "you *have* got a heap of education comin' to you! That's tar soap, son, the pitchman's friend."

Doubtful, Hassle applied the tar soap to the clean axle and hub. "I never heard of greasin' a wheel with soap before."

"Lot of things you never heard about, son. Get plenty of that on the axle now. Smear her around good."

Within a matter of minutes Hassle had everything covered with tar soap. "Fine!" California Sam said happily. "Now put the wheel back on and we'll be ready to make our pitch."

Hassle put the wheel back on the axle, slapped the hub in place and tightened it down. "Is that all?"

"Course that's all, boy," Sam told him impatiently. "Put that jack back in the equipment box and let's get started."

As Sam drove into town the sodbusters came out of the stores and stared at the gaudily decorated wagon. The pitchman nudged Hassle, grinning. "Look at 'em! They're already suckered and they ain't even heard my pitch yet. You think you can handle a team of mules?"

"I been drivin' mules since I was old enough to hold the lines."

"Here," Sam told him without further ado, and thrust the lines into the boy's hands. "Drive her down to the end of the street, then bring her around smart and come to a stop." He swept off his widebrim beaver hat and waved to the natives. "Like takin' candy right out of the hands of a trustin' infant," he said to Hassle from the side of his mouth. "Howdy, sir! Howdy, ma'am! Just foller the wagon, folks, there's goin' to be a free show!"

To Hassle's amazement, California reached into the wagon, hauled out a five string banjo and began to sing "Buffalo Gal" at the top of his voice. The yokels poured out of the stores. They followed the wagon to the end of the street, then, when Hassle smartly reversed himself and came to a halt, they almost trampled each other in their excitement.

As soon as the wagon lurched to a halt, Sam grabbed Hassle's shoulder and said under his breath. "Look smart now, boy. Get down there and unhitch them mules. Let down that rear platform, fill the torches with coal oil and put them in the side brackets. I'll do everything else." A heavy-set, red-faced man with a hostile look about him was shoving his way through the crowd. "Oh, oh," said Sam, with a sigh of resignation. "I was scared somethin' like this would happen."

"Somethin' like what?" Hassle asked, slightly dazed.

"Here comes the law, boy. Nickel-plated badge, six-shootin' revolver and all. Well, there ain't nothin' for it. I've got to make a fix."

"What with?" the boy demanded. "You ain't got any money, have you?"

"There's ways, boy. There's ways."

By this time the town marshal of Plateau, Oklahoma Territory, a rather excitable and overweight gentleman whose name was Burt Hazzlet, had climbed up on the front wheel and had California Sam by his tasseled sleeve. "Look here, what're you tryin' to pull, mister? We don't allow the sellin' of medicine, or peddlin' of any kind, inside the city limits of Plateau, without you got a license."

"That goes without sayin', sir," Sam told him with dignity. "California Sam ain't exactly what you'd call a greenhorn. I know all about licenses and such." He removed the man's hand from his buckskin sleeve. "Kindly show me the way to the mayor, sir, and I'll attend to this little detail right away."

Marshal Burt Hazzlet looked disappointed that the pitchman had given in without an argument. Sam was familiar with the situation. The town of Plateau had probably just built itself a brand-new rock calaboose and couldn't wait to see somebody in it. "Well, all right," the lawman said sourly. "Get down and foller me."

Sam did as he was instructed, but not before waving again to the crowd and hollering, "The free show will commence in just a few minutes, folks! Just as soon as my assistant sets up the platform!" To Marshal Hazzlet he said from the side of his mouth, "Let us get started! Not even a yokel will stand in one spot forever!"

As the lawman plowed his way back through the crowd, Sam followed in his dusty wake, grinning and waving to the gaping natives. He didn't have the slightest notion how he was going to pay for a license, and for the moment he refused to worry about it. With an experienced eye he sized up the crowd and was pleased to note that a good one third of the number was women. He had never seen a crowd riper for the Wa-Hoe Miracle Soap pitch.

The two men stepped up to the dirt sidewalk and Sam followed the marshal into a small general store. The place was crowded with all kinds of merchandise, as were all general stores, but amazingly uncluttered with customers. The only person in the store was a small intense, fiercely scowling man who looked as if he might be approaching the edge of apoplexy.

"This here," the marshal said to Sam, "is Otis Mott. Otis is the mayor hereabouts."

Sam beamed and grabbed Mayor Mott's hand and wrung it heartily. He knew exactly how to handle Otis. "Mr. Mayor," he shouted into the man's astonished face, "it's a great honor to meet up with you. There's been a slight misunderstandin' with your marshal here, but nothin' that can't be straightened out in just a few minutes."

"Misunderstandin'!" Marshal Hazzlet sounded as if he had been stabbed. "There ain't no misunderstandin' about it, Mayor! He was tryin' to sell medicine inside the city limits without a license!"

Sam smiled warmly at the two of them. "I'm sorry to dispute with an officer of the law, Mayor, but he's mistook my intentions. My intentions, sir, wasn't to sell nothin' at all. Not a *thing*, your honor. All I aimed to do was to try to entertain those good, hard-workin' folks out there . . ."

The mayor's fuse had finally burned down. "You emptied my store of customers!" he hollered. "That's what you done!"

"Only for a little while, Mayor," Sam said soothingly, overwhelming him with sheer good will and brotherly concern. "And I'm tellin' you the honest truth. I don't aim to sell a thing. No medicine, no herbs, no electric oil, no soaps or salves. Nothin'."

Sam beamed benignly. "You're right, your honor. I *do*

have a business proposition to put to you, if you'd like to listen for a minute." He smiled at the marshal. "In private."

Otis Mott's every instinct told him to run this charlatan out of town immediately before he could say another word. Still, business was business. Curiosity and greed overcame him. "Burt," he said to the marshal, "get out there and see that nothin' gets sold without I give the word." When he was alone with the pitchman he pulled himself up and said with a sneer, "All right, just how do you aim to make a profit if you don't sell nothin'?"

"Easy," California Sam grinned. "You do the sellin' for me."

Otis Mott thought about that for a minute, his face frozen, his eyes like bullets. At last he nodded. "Go on."

"I make my pitch, like always. When the yokels—the customers—are in the right frame of mind for buyin', I tell them I can't sell them the merchandise myself, but they can come in here and buy it from you. You do the sellin' and gather in the cash. We divvy up fifty-fifty."

"Cash!" Mayor Mott's mouth turned down as he said it. "You don't reckon a store in a new territory does business for cash, do you? I have to carry these folks on my books. That costs money. We divvy up sixty-forty."

Sam's smile of good will never flickered. It was always a pleasure doing business with men of greed, they were so easy to cheat. "Mayor, whatever you make on the deal comes free and clear. No expenses, no risk. All you do is take in the money."

Mott set his steel-trap jaw. "Sixty-forty."

"Fifty-five, forty-five."

"No." The mayor shook his head stubbornly.

"Take it or leave it." Sam waited a minute and then turned and started to walk out of the store.

"I can have you arrested for entertainin' without a license!"

"I haven't done any entertainin' yet."

"I heard you singin' when you drove into town. That's entertainin'."

Sam sighed to himself. Yes sir, this was going to be a pleasure. "All right, Mayor, I guess you got me. Sixty-forty."

"We don't divvy up till after I collect the money."

"That's what I said, Mayor, and California Sam's a man of his word."

"One more thing. Just what is it you're sellin'?"

"Soap, Mayor. Wa-Hoe Miracle Soap."

Otis Mott pulled a sour face, as if he had been insulted. "You're out of your head! I got a store full of soap. Venus, Pear's, Wild Rose, P & G, Oakley's. You name it, I already got it here in the store."

"You ain't got Wa-Hoe Miracle Soap," Sam told him with a grin.

"What's so special about Wa-Hoe whatever you call it?"

"Listen to my pitch, Mayor, and you'll find out."

By the time Sam got back to the wagon, Hassle had unhitched the mules, let down the platform, filled the torches and put them in the brackets. Sam looked the situation over and rubbed his hands with satisfaction. "Let's get started! Light the torches, boy!"

"Did you make the fix?"

California Sam noted with some pride that the boy was beginning to talk like a pitchman. "Easiest thing in the world, son, I almost feel ashamed of myself, it was so easy."

Sam waited until the coal oil-filled torches were burning, then he mounted the platform. A high pitchman would no more pitch without his torches than a cowhand would venture out of doors without his Stetson. The suckers, as he was pleased to see, were waiting patiently for the free show that had been promised them.

The pitchman swept off his widebrim beaver, scanned the male faces looking up at him from ground level. "Gentlemen," he said with dignity, "will please remove their hats. We got to remember at all times that there's ladies present today."

The men looked stunned. For a while the womenfolks only stared blankly at the buckskin-class stranger on the platform. Then they turned and began to look at one another and smile. Probably it was the first time in a long while that any deference had been shown them—for some it could have been the first time in their lives. The men, not knowing quite what to do, shifted from foot to foot. At last a townsman, grinning self-consciously, took off his dented plug hat and held it awkwardly in both hands. One by one the other men uncovered and allowed the hot afternoon sun to beat on their heads.

California Sam beamed at them. He considered this an excellent sign, for he knew that getting a yokel's hat off his head was often more difficult than getting money out of his pocket. With a startling whoop that caused some of the womenfolks to jump, the pitchman grabbed up his banjo and began a lively chorus of "The Sow Took the Measles."

From the edge of the crowd Hassle watched in astonishment as Sam tore through the song with professional flare. Soon the yokels were patting their feet and raising a knee-high ground fog of dust all around the platform. Hassle watched pleased grins come to their weathered faces as Sam broke off between choruses to do a lively jig while still plucking the banjo.

Abruptly Sam shifted to "I've Got No Use for Women," and the menfolks nodded their heads knowingly, and the ladies smiled and looked smug. The pitchman shifted again to "The Streets of Laredo," and within a matter of minutes there wasn't a completely dry eye in the crowd. He followed it up with "The Rosewood Casket," and the womenfolks began crying openly.

Then, to Hassle's further amazement, California Sam put the banjo down, clapped his hands sharply, like a magician at the climax of a disappearing act, and changed the crowd's mood completely. He reached into the wagon and took out a length of hemp rope. Instantly the rope was a live, soaring thing in his hands. He shook out a large, flat loop, and the natives—some of them cowhands from nearby Indian Territory—stared bug-eyed as the loop expanded and contracted, jumped and slithered. "Here's the ocean wave!" the pitchman announced, and the yokels' heads went up and down following the oceanlike gyrations of the rope. "The wedding ring!" Sam hollered, and the loop soared straight up and came down around his waist.

Although the pitchman's world was a new one to Hassle Jones, the boy realized that he was witnessing ballyhoo of a high order. He watched spellbound as California Sam took up a shorter length of rope and began tying knots faster than the eye could follow. A simple bend, a sheet bend, a carrick bend. A hitch, a half hitch, a figure eight hitch, two half hitches, and a slipped half hitch.

With timing that bordered on genius, Sam stopped the rope tricks while the natives' mouths were still hanging open. He put the rope aside and stood for a moment, gazing into space. Without actually doing a thing he had changed the mood for the third time.

Silently, the suckers waited to see what he would do next. For a full minute Sam stared into space, and finally he said quietly, "Ladies and Gentlemen, there will be more entertainment later, but right now, with your kind permission, I would like to be serious for a moment. And again, with your kind permission, I would like to talk a little about myself, and about some friends of mine, a tribe of savage Wa-Hoe Indians who reside in those towering, all but inaccessible mountains in faraway California . . ."

It occurred to Hassle that here was gall of a special class, using Indians to ballyhoo a group of yokels who rubbed elbows with Indians every day.

But the sodbusters didn't seem to notice. They allowed California Sam to lead them into the pitch, and almost immediately they were hooked. "As a young man," Sam started slowly, "it was my passion to hunt the fierce grizzly bear in those great California mountains where the Wa-Hoes make their home. One day when I was out hunting I came across a small Indian boy who had been terribly mauled by a bear. He was near death . . ."

Hassle had heard the lecture twice before, once by torchlight in front of Omar's Western Trail Saloon in Wichita, once at the Wichita wagon yard where Hassle had been hiding in the medicine man's wagon. Still, he found himself leaning forward as the white hunter's adventures among the Wa-Hoes began to take shape. He found himself straining to hear every word for fear that he might miss something of unimaginable importance. It was exactly the same lecture that Hassle had heard on the other two occasions—Sam had memorized it word for word exactly as the San Francisco newspaperman had written it.

For some minutes the pitchman dealt lovingly with the exceptional beauty of the savage Wa-Hoe tribesmen, especially the lushness and gloss of their hair. Hassle realized that for a moment it had slipped Sam's mind just what it was he was selling that day. He was about to plunge into the Electric Hair Restorer pitch when he suddenly pulled up short, gazed thoughtfully out at the crowd and said, "I wonder if any of you listening to the sound of my voice knows what it's like to be clean?"

If any yokel had allowed his mind to wander, the pitchman's query hauled him quickly into line. Some of the men cocked their heads, blinked several times and wondered if they had heard correctly. Some of the women were beginning to look outraged.

Sam raised his hand in a fatherly gesture and smiled. "Oh, I don't mean to imply that there's anybody in this crowd that don't wash good every day, regular as clockwork.

Lookin' down at your sensitive, intelligent faces, I *know* that you do. But do you get *clean*? That's the question we want to investigate today, my friends . . ."

Young Hassle Jones—an eleven-year-old boy well on his way to becoming a cynic—wanted to laugh at the stunned look on the sodbusters' faces. They looked like so many shipwrecked victims floundering on a limitless ocean.

California Sam threw them a lifeline. He backtracked and worked the Miracle Soap, not the Electric Hair Restorer, into the pitch. It was the Miracle Soap, manufactured according to a secret formula known only to Wa-Hoe medicine men, that accounted for the exceptional beauty of that savage people. With that point cleared up, Sam shifted gears again.

He took a paper-wrapped object from his pocket and held it up for all to see. "You all know what this is," he said with a smile, as one well bred, knowledgeable person to another. "It is a bar of soap. Common, ordinary soap, the kind you find in stores everywhere. To be more specific," he said, glancing at the label, "it is a bar of Pale Olive, good for general household use as well as the feminine complexion." He lowered his voice and smiled again, knowingly. "*If* we are to believe what it says on the label!"

The women looked vaguely worried. Most of them had a bar of Pale Olive in the soap dish on the washstand at home and used it regularly. "Have you ever wondered," Sam went on in a confidential tone, "what the folks that make Pale Olive put *in* their soap?"

Hassle, somewhat to his own disgust, found himself shaking his head along with all the other yokels.

The pitchman, with the air of a man who has a great deal of bad news to get off his chest, heaved a sigh. "Well," he continued, "I'm sure all of you have seen the advertisements in the commercial section of the newspapers. 'Top prices paid for dead horses.' Or, 'Highest prices paid for dead cows.' Do you know who it is that's payin' top prices for these dead animals?" He paused for effect, then shouted, "The soapmakers! That's who!"

There was an audible gasp from some of the women. Sam hit them again while they were still dazed. "That's where those poor dead and diseased animals wind up, folks, in the soapmaking vats! And that's just the beginnin'. Have you ever wondered what the butchers do with the scraps of tainted meat and rancid fat that they can't sell to their customers? They sell it to the soapmakers! Have you ever wondered what happens to the barrels of spoiled meat and garbage that accumulates in hotels and restaurants? Yes sir, I see you noddin' your heads out there, and you're absolutely right—it goes to the people that make your soap that you use at home. All this time you've been wonderin' what happens to all the dead sheep and goats and cows and horses. Well, now you know. And dogs! What do you think the dogcatcher does with faithful old Spot when he catches him and takes him off to the pound? You're absolutely right, ma'am, I see you noddin' your head—old Spot winds up in the soapmakin' vat along with all the others!"

There was a look of rising anger on the yokels' faces as they stared up at the pitchman. In another few minutes they would be ready to go out and lynch somebody.

"Friends," Sam told them with infinite sadness, "it ain't my intention to shock you but to tell you the truth. And the truth ain't always pretty. The soapmakers take all these poor dead animals, the sheep and the pigs and the cows and horses. They put them in a big cookin' vat, along with old Spot and maybe a few cats, and they cook them down. They take the fat and bleach it with strong acids, and it's saponified with lye and caustic soda and potash. They throw in a little cheap perfume to make it smell good. And there you have it. Soap. Just like this bar I'm holdin' in my hand. Well, I'm sure it don't come to you as any big surprise that women who use this kind of soap on their faces get old before their time. It won't surprise the menfolks that their hands get so dry and cracked that it's hard to do a good day's work. It ain't any wonder that cancer of the skin has become the curse of humanity. Think of the soap that goes on that skin. Even little children are affected by the use of these soaps. Did you ever see a child that wasn't afflicted with blackheads and pimples and maybe even boils? I ask you, right this minute, to turn your heads and take a good look at your neighbor. Does his skin look harsh and dry and scaly? Is the poor soul cursed with blackheads and pimples? Are his hands dry and cracked around the knuckles? Is his hair falling out?"

The suckers turned and studied their neighbors. What they saw appalled them. Sure enough, there was hardly a person in the crowd who didn't show signs of rapid degeneration due to extensive use of commercial soap.

"Well, friends," Sam told them sorrowfully, "there ain't no use goin' on about the big soapmakers in our country. They make soap for profit, and naturally they use the cheapest ingredients they can lay their hands on. If faithful old Spot or the family cow winds up in the soapmaker's vat, it means a few more pieces of silver in the pockets of big businessmen . . ."

Sam took out a bandanna and patted his forehead. He glanced up at the sun and guessed that it was less than three hours till sundown. With luck he might hold the sodbusters for another hour, then they would have to get back to their homesteads for the nightly milking and other chores. It was time to wind up the pitch.

"Well," he told them, "you can see by lookin' at my outfit that I ain't a businessman. No use to worry about old Spot turnin' up missin' when I pull out of town. And like I told you when I first drove into your fair little city, I don't aim to try to sell you anything. Not a thing. But, with your kind permission, I would like to tell you a few things about a soap that the old Wa-Hoe medicine men make back in those big mountains in California."

He flung away the poisonous bar of Pale Olive. From his pocket he took out a small square of Miracle Soap and held it up for them to see. The sunlight glinted on its tinfoil wrapping. He gazed at it reverently.

"Friends," Sam told them in round sincere tones, "I hold in my hands a bar of Indian Soap. The Miracle Soap of the Wa-Hoe Indians. I can see that some of you are not impressed. It is small, much smaller than the bars of common soap that you buy in stores. But it ain't the size that determines the value of a thing—if it was, a diamond ring would sell for less than a stick of hoarhound candy. No sir, it ain't the size that counts." He took the tinfoil wrapping off the soap and let them look at it. "There it is. Looks pretty much the same as a common bar of white soap, don't it? But let me tell you, ladies and gentlemen, there's a world of difference between Wa-Hoe Miracle Soap and any other soap you ever laid eyes on before!"

The suckers stared open-mouthed at the small piece of soap. "I wish I could tell you all the things that went into this little piece of Miracle Soap," Sam told them regretfully, "but I can't. I took a blood oath to Ho-Wa-Wa, the great chief of the Wa-Hoes, that I would never tell a livin' soul. I *can* tell you that nothin' goes into this soap but *natural* ingredients. No fat from diseased animals. No harsh acids to dry and crack your skin. *Natural* ingredients, friends, that's the secret of this wonderful soap, perfumed only with rare herbs that the Wa-Hoes grow especially for that purpose."

California Sam paused for a moment, staring at some particular spot near the edge of the crowd. "I see you shakin' your head, sir. Soap's soap, you say. What's so different from this little bar in my hand and the soap you've been buyin'? Well, sir, there's plenty difference, but I don't expect you to take it on faith. City businessmen bamboozle us every day makin' fancy claims for their product that they can't back up. I don't blame you for bein' suspicious. But stay a little longer, my friend, and pay close attention, because California Sam ain't your common run businessman. When California Sam tells you a thing, he backs it up with proof!"

The pitchman pulled himself up tall and glared at the sea of yokel faces. "*Proof!*" he shouted at them. Then, in a quieter tone he continued, "But first I'd be honored to speak to the ladies for a few minutes."

Sam beamed down at the sodbuster women. After a moment of startled blankness, the women began to smile. "The girls and women," he told them confidentially, "of the Wa-Hoe tribe, don't have special preparations to make their hair thick and lustrous. They don't have hot irons to make it curly. All they have is this soap and the Lord's pure rainwater. They take this soap and wash their hair in rainwater once every week or so. That's all. Work up a good lather with the Miracle Soap and then give it a good rinsing. It won't take more than ten minutes of your time, and I never seen a Wa-Hoe woman that didn't have the shiniest, thickest, most naturally curly hair that a body ever looked at!" In an aside to the men, "Now that I think about it, I never seen a Wa-Hoe man that didn't have a good thick head of hair on him. I don't *know* if the men wash their hair in Miracle Soap, but I guess it stands to reason."

The bald men in the crowd, whose unhatted scalps were beginning to turn pink beneath the afternoon sun, listened attentively.

"And complexion!" Sam exclaimed, suddenly turning back to the women. "One of the first things I noticed about Wa-Hoe women was their complexion, smooth as cream and not a blemish. Then I learned that the womenfolks of the tribe wash their faces every day with *Miracle* Soap. If a blemish *should* appear, the woman simply works up a little lather, puts it on the place and gently rubs it in until the soap is no longer visible. The next day the blemish is gone.

In especially stubborn cases," he added, by way of insurance to himself, "the treatment may have to be repeated."

Sam glanced again at the sun. It was time to start winding up. "Babies," he said to the sodbuster women. "When you put baby in the dishpan to give him a washing, what does he do? He cries! Of course he cries, that harsh soap, full of acids and sick animal fat, is burnin' his skin. Wa-Hoe Miracle Soap won't burn his skin, because it's *pure*. Nothin' but natural ingredients all down the line. Why, if a body happened to have an appetite for soap he could eat Miracle Soap and it would not hurt him in the slightest."

Because of the dwindling time Sam quickly passed over the many other advantages of using Wa-Hoe Miracle Soap, but he did mention that it made an excellent shaving soap, that it was a sure cure for cracked skin, eczema, perspiring and aching feet, among other human afflictions.

The time had arrived for the *punch.*

Sam gazed out at his audience with a hurt look on his homely face. "I see that some of you are still not sure about Wa-Hoe Miracle Soap. You say, sure, it may be a fine soap for the hair and complexion, but it's a very little bar and it's probably expensive. And, you say, after all, a soap is made for *cleanin'* things. That's its main purpose. Can a soap mild enough to bathe the baby with be strong enough to do regular household work? Would it be economical to buy such a small bar of soap like this one when you can buy a much larger bar in any store for half the price. Ladies and gentlemen, I say those are fair questions and they ought to have fair answers. And I intend to *give* you those answers!"

He gestured to Hassle, and the boy made his way through the crowd to the platform. "Get the canvas bucket under the driver's seat," Sam told him, "and fetch me some water from the town pump."

Hassle, feeling that all eyes had turned on him, took the bucket and swaggered to the pump at the end of the street. When he returned, Sam took the bucket and said to the audience, "Friends, I'll now ask my young assistant to get the wagon jack and appropriate wrenches and remove one of the wheels from the wagon. Is there a strong young man in the audience that'll volunteer to give the lad a helpin' hand?"

A sheepish young sodbuster stepped forward. "I don't mind."

"Excellent!" California Sam beamed down at him. Hassle and the sodbuster went to work on the wheel—Hassle didn't have to be told which wheel. Within a matter of minutes they had the wheel off and passed it up to Sam on the platform.

The pitchman regarded the wheel with extreme distaste. "Did you ever see an uglier sight than that, folks? A wheel full of axle grease is about the messiest thing there is, I guess, and about the hardest thing to clean. Is there anybody in the crowd that wants to dispute my word on that?"

Apparently, nobody was eager for that honor. The natives stared at the great globs of black substance that oozed between the spokes and wondered what he was going to do about it. "Hold on!" Sam hollered at an invisible yokel at the rear of the crowd. "Don't go yet, I know you think it's goin' to take me the rest of the day and a good part of the night to get a wheel like this clean—but I've got a little surprise in store for you. Just a few minutes, that's all I ask."

Apparently the imaginary doubter decided to stay and see it through, for Sam smiled at him warmly. "Now," he said briskly, "we'll get down to business and see what this little bar of Miracle Soap can do. But first I want to prove to you that everything's honest and aboveboard. No flimflam from California Sam!" Then, dramatically, he lifted the bucket, put to his mouth and drank from it. "Pure water!" he said sternly, wiping his mouth. "Nothin' but pure water. If anybody in the crowd believes I'm goin' to use doctored water to clean this wheel with, just let him step up and have a swaller hisself."

The bareheaded men were beginning to look hot and thirsty, but no one stepped forward to accept the pitchman's invitation. "Very well!" Sam told them happily. "We'll get started then! I'll just dip this sponge into the water like this." Into the water bucket went the sponge that he had so carefully loaded with soap. "Then I'll give her a swipe or two on this little bar of Wa-Hoe Miracle Soap." Lightly, he stroked the sponge across the small piece of soap. "Looky there!" California Sam exclaimed. "See them suds! See all them suds!"

The startled group of natives gave an audible gasp as a veritable ocean of white suds foamed up from the small sponge. In less than a minute the pitchman was up to his elbows in suds. He grasped the wheel firmly and went to work on the black, gummy mess in the hub cavity. More suds boiled out of the sponge. Sam grinned down at the yokels and hummed a happy little tune as he worked. After two or three minutes the soap in the sponge, combined with the tar soap—an effective cleaning agent in spite of its appearance—continued to boil over on the platform. Sam was up to his ankles in suds, and still they came. Suds dripped off the platform onto the ground, and the yokels slunk away from it, as if it had been witches brew.

When Sam had the "axle grease" reduced completely to pure suds, he took a clean rag, and, with a flourish, wiped the wheel clean. One of the watch-owning yokels shouted, "Three minutes! Three minutes on the dot!"

The pitchman grinned widely. "Thank you, friend, but I ain't through yet. There's the axle to clean yet. See that axle, folks? Did you ever see a greasier, messier thing in your life? Well, we'll fix that up in just a minute." Wading through a great mound of suds, he stepped to the edge of the platform and handed the dripping sponge down to Hassle. "I'm goin' to let my young assistant work on that axle, folks, just to prove there ain't no cleanin' job so tough that a child can't do it. As long as he's got a bar of Wa-Ho Miracle Soap!"

A surprised Hassle accepted the bubbling sponge. He was beginning to realize that it paid to be prepared for the unexpected when you traveled with a man like California Sam.

The suckers crowded in close to see if a mere boy could actually clean up that messy-looking axle, even with the aid of Wa-Hoe Miracle Soap. Hassle attacked his job with a will. He rubbed and scrubbed until the axle gleamed and the ground all around him was covered with quivering mounds of suds. "Two minutes!" the yokel with the watch hollered. There was even some handclapping and whistling.

California Sam mentally patted himself on the back–it had been a shrewd move involving the boy in the pitch. Rare was the yokel who did not look favorably on the efforts of a child. That was something to remember and think about.

4

THE sodbusters were sold. They began ganging around the platform, some of them with pieces of silver in their hands. California Sam, still standing ankle-deep in the miraculous suds, held up his hand and announced with great dignity: "Friends, that little demonstration was just by way of entertainment. You'll recollect that I said, when I first got up on this platform, that I wouldn't try to sell you anything from the wagon. That was the word of California Sam. It was the truth. However, if you are convinced that these little bars of Wa-Hoe Miracle Soap are everything I've claimed for them, you can step over to Mayor Mott's store and buy directly from him. I hope you liked our little show. Goodbye and God bless you all!"

The male sodbusters put their hats on their broiled heads. They looked stunned from the demonstration and the relentlessness of California Sam's lecturing. Before they knew what was happening, the ladies were hazing them toward Otis Mott's store.

Sam ducked into the wagon, gathered a tomato crate full of wrapped and labled Miracle Soap and handed it down to Hassle. "Take this to Mott in a hurry! Better go around through the back door. Tell him to charge whatever he thinks right; he knows his customers better'n I do."

Sam took the mules to the wagon yard and got them a rubdown and a good feed. In a few minutes Hassle came into the barn grinning widely. "You ought to see 'em! The farmers are buyin' that Miracle Soap like it was the only soap there was!"

"Farmers?" Sam looked at the boy as if he had been speaking a foreign tongue. "You mean sodbusters. Of course they're buyin' it. Why shouldn't they? It was a good pitch."

"How did I do? Did I clean that axle to suit you?"

"You cleaned it fine," Sam told him with a generous wave of his hand. "Which reminds me. You better get back to the wagon and put the wheel back on with real grease this time."

It was around midnight when Dutch Rainey's horse stumbled over an outcrop and almost went down. Dutch could feel the trembling of the big sorrel's shoulders. There was nothing for it now; the animal had to be rested or soon it would simply fall down and die.

An enraged Dutch Rainey with a cracking and bleeding scalp, made dry camp on the prairie for the rest of the night. He soaked his bandanna with water from his canteen and put it on his head. It did nothing to cool his rage, but it did ease the demoniac itching for a little while. He chewed some jerky and drank some water and went to sleep.

By morning the sorrel was looking a little better, but Dutch knew that the animal would not last much longer. Well, if the sorrel played out, he would have to get another horse. Even if it meant stealing one. For by this time the meaning of his entire life had boiled down to a single fact, and that fact was beautifully clear in its implicity—Dutch Rainey was going to catch a certain medicine show doc by the name of California Sam. And then he was going to kill him.

Near midday he stopped at a sodbuster's dugout to water the sorrel and see what he could find out. The sodbuster hadn't seen anybody called California Sam, but he had heard that a medicine show man had stopped the day before in Plateau. That was about five miles on to the west, the farmer allowed. Right on the road to Pond Creek.

Dutch was cheered by this piece of news. With a little luck he would reach Plateau before the pitchman got away. He pulled the sorrel's cinch in a notch, raked the animal's flanks with his spurs and struck west.

The sun was little more than an hour high when the last sodbuster wagon rattled out of Plateau. "Hitch up the mules," California Sam told his youthful assistant. "Get ready to pull out as soon as I settle with the storekeeper."

Hassle pulled a sour face. "I was thinkin' maybe we'd stay in town for the night. With all the money you're goin' to get from old Mott, I figgered we'd eat supper in the cafe."

"You figgered wrong," the pitchman told him bluntly. "Get the mules hitched if you aim to travel on with me." He started out of the barn, then hesitated at the door and said, "Wait a minute. How much was the mayor chargin' the suckers for that Miracle Soap?"

Hassle grinned. "Four bits, straight down the line. I hung around until I was sure. Figgered you'd want to know."

Yes sir, Sam thought to himself. The boy was showing promise.

Otis Mott was dazedly writing up the sales in an account book when Sam entered the store. "I don't believe it!" he said, shaking his head. "They bought every bar of that soap! Do you know how many there were?"

"Exactly," Sam told him with a grin. "One hundred bars."

That took the edge off of Mott's pleasure—he had been on the verge of claiming ninety bars, or maybe even eighty. "One hundred," he said after a moment, his mouth pursed as if he had bitten into a green persimmon. "Yes, I guess you're here to settle up. Sixty-forty, you said."

"*You* said," Sam told him cheerfully. "But that's all right. I ain't greedy."

Mott shot him a narrow glance, then hauled out a cash-box and began counting greenbacks. "Let's see, at a quarter a bar, forty percent would be . . ."

"Four bits a bar," Sam told him with a good natured smile.

They locked glances for a moment. For an instant it occurred to the mayor to stand his ground and double his profit. But there was a certain glint in the pitchman's watery eyes that tempered his natural greed. He pretended to squint closely at his account book. "An honest mistake," he said grudgingly. "Four bits. A hundred bars, that's fifty dollars. Your part comes to twenty dollars."

"Much oblige, Mayor," Sam beamed. He took the well-worn greenbacks, stuffed them in his pocket and waited for Mayor Mott to make his next move.

"Ahhh . . ." the mayor said, gazing into the distance. "I was just thinkin'. If you had some more of that soap that you wanted to get off your hands. Of course, I'd have to keep it on my shelf for a long time. I couldn't pay much."

"How much?" Sam asked absently, filling his corncob pipe.

"Say fifteen cents a bar."

"Say a quarter a bar."

"Twenty. That's as high as I'll go."

"Mayor," Sam told him with feeling, "you got yourself another hundred bars of Wa-Hoe Miracle Soap!"

Back at the wagon yard Sam spent several minutes cutting large ten-cent bars of soap into small fifty-cent bars, wrapping them in tinfoil and sticking them with Wa-Hoe labels.

"If I hadn't seen it with my own eyes," Otis Mott said, as Sam dumped the merchandise on his counter, "I would never of believed it. It don't seem possible that such a little bit of soap could clean a wheel of axle grease!"

"Queer things go on in the world, Mayor," Sam told him with a wide smile.

He returned to the wagon with a bottle of Kentucky whiskey, a wedge of yellow cheese, two cans of sardines, and a pound of crackers. "We'll eat on the road," he told his young assistant. "There's somethin' about this place. It's givin' me the itch to travel."

"Did you sell the rest of that soap to the mayor?"

"Sure I did, boy. You don't think I cut and wrapped all them bars for nothin', do you?"

"Then I reckon you can afford to pay me my dollar."

"Son," Sam told him with an absent-minded pat on the head, "you're a good enough boy, but it ain't seemly for a young'un to pester folks about money all the time."

They traveled southeast until almost dark. From time to time Sam would look back over his shoulder, scanning their backtrail. Dusk came down, hot and dry, on the prairie. The pitchman fell into a vague mood of uneasiness. His skin prickled. He kept scratching the back of his neck.

Young Hassle Jones had been watching the curious actions of his companion for some time. At last he said, "You ain't scared them sodbusters will come after us wantin' their money back, are you?"

Sam shook his head. "Nothin' like that. As a matter of fact that's a first-class cleanin' soap they bought. Little expensive, maybe, but that'll make them use it more careful. The women'll give their faces a careful cleanin' and their complexions'll get better, just like I told them. They wash their hair with rainwater and it'll look clean and shiny, like I said it would. If they got achin' feet, they soak their feet in hot water and rub on a little Miracle Soap, and their feet'll feel better."

"What if they try to clean axle grease off a wagon wheel?"

"What fool would try to do a thing like that?" the pitchman asked irritably. "That was all flash. Not even a yokel would waste expensive Wa-Hoe Miracle Soap cleanin' up a wagon wheel."

"Well," the youth said doggedly, "somethin's frettin' you. You been twistin' and turnin' ever since we pulled out of town."

With ill temper, California Sam uncorked the bottle of Kentucky whiskey. "Open up them cans of sardines," he told the boy. "We'll travel on a while before we camp."

They made dry camp that night somewhere between Red Creek and the Little Arkansas. The hours passed quietly, but the pitchman was in a sour mood when he roused himself the next morning.

"Look out for that fire," he barked at Hassle, who was boiling Arbuckle's beside the wagon. "You want to start the whole prairie to burnin'?" Then he saw that the boy had dug a trench to build his cookfire; an old-time plainsman couldn't have done it better. But he didn't bother to apologize.

They ate breakfast in silence. The boy watched his companion with narrowed eyes, and at last the pitchman became aware that he was being watched. Sam managed a small grin. "I don't aim to holler at you, boy."

"That's all right," Hassle told him. "I been hollered at before."

"Well, when we get to Pond Creek I'll put you on the train and send you back to Wichita. This ain't no kind of life for a young'un."

The youth said nothing for several minutes. He began stirring around, cleaning the plates and skillet, putting out the fire. "It don't seem like such a bad life to me," he said at last. "I was all right yesterday, wasn't I? Settin' up your outfit, helpin' you with your pitch?"

"You done fine," the pitchman told him. "All the same, you ought to be back with your folks. You're too young to be on the road."

By the time the morning sun had cleared the eastern horizon they had the wagon back on the road again. With a little luck, Sam thought, they would raise Pond Creek around dark. It would be good to see a live town again. He decided that a railroad town would be about right for the Wa-Hoe Indian Herb Mixture pitch. The profit on herbs was not as big as that in Miracle Soap and Electric Hair Restorer; on the other hand, the pitchman could take his time and stay in a place for several days if he felt like it. Herbs were safe. California Sam bought them from wholesale drug companies—Alexandria senna, cascara bark, Cape aloes, sassafras, sugar, baking soda, barberis root, and star aniseed—and mixed them himself in a little alcohol and water. It was a first-class physic, and there was nothing a yokel had more faith in than a good physic.

The pitchman began to feel a little more at ease. With any kind of luck he ought to make a hundred—maybe two hundred—dollars at Pond Creek. Then he'd move on down the track to Oklahoma City. It had been a long time since he had been in a town of that size. A few months ago there had been a bit of trouble in Denver—a small matter of a police sergeant and a Wa-Hoe Electric Belt. The Electric Belt, a "cure" for any kidney or back ailment a yokel might imagine he had, relied on a preparation of zinc and vinegar for its effect. The trouble with zinc and vinegar was that they sometimes raised a sore, like a saddle gall, on the sucker's back, which sometimes accounted for considerable unpleasantness all around. At any rate, Sam had left Denver one night as fast as his mules could pull the wagon, and he hadn't seen the inside of a real city since.

Around midmorning a dry, hot wind rose in the east. It made an eerie, moaning sound as it bent the brown heads of prairie grass. Sam's pleasant mood began to wear thin. The hot July sun beat down on his head. The heat was dry and prickly and alive with electricity.

Hassle dozed on the seat next to the pitchman. From time to time he would twitch and make strange small sounds in his throat. Dreaming, California Sam thought to himself. He wondered idly what a boy of eleven years old could have to dream about.

Once the youth cried out. Sam couldn't make heads or tails out of what he was saying, but for a moment Hassle lurched up in the seat, his face almost white, his teeth bared like a young wolf. Alarmed, the pitchman grabbed him by the shoulder and shook him. "Wake up, boy! What in damnation's ailin' you?"

The boy came awake with a start. His fists clinched, he stared at Sam with blazing eyes. The pitchman let go of his shoulder. "Gentle down, son," he said quietly. "Everything's all right. Nobody's goin' to hurt you."

Hassle licked his dry lips. "I ain't afraid!"

"Nobody said you was. You dozed off and had a bad dream, that's all."

The boy breathed deeply several times. He looked out at the great tawny sea of grass, like a sailor in strange waters trying to get his bearings. At last he began to relax. "Whereabouts are we?"

"Not too far from Red Creek, accordin' to this map. We ought to be raisin' the town of Pond Creek by nightfall."

For sometime they rode in silence. Suddenly the youth said, "I ain't goin' back to Wichita!"

The pitchman shrugged. "All right, I won't try to make you. But what have you got against Wichita?"

"I ain't goin' back, that's all!" Then, after a little while: "I'll leave you at Pond Creek, if that's what you want. I won't be a bother any more."

"Gentle down, son," the pitchman told him again. "The sun's too hot to go gettin' yourself in a sweat. You can do whatever you want to do, it don't make any difference to me."

It was about an hour later when they first glimpsed the distant figure moving, almost imperceptibly, along the huge curve of the horizon. "Hell and damnation!" the pitchman exclaimed, nudging Hassle with his elbow. "Your eyes're sharper'n mine are. What do you make out of that?"

Since his brief outburst Hassle had been riding stiffly beside his companion, his arms folded across his chest, as silent as a Kiowa. Now he fixed his gaze on the distant figure and shrugged his thin shoulders. "Somebody afoot."

"Hell of a place to be afoot," Sam said irritably. "Can you tell what he looks like?"

The boy squinted for several seconds. "Looks like a woman," he said at last.

California Sam stared at him. "What would a woman be doin' afoot in the middle of the bald prairie?"

"I don't know. But it's a woman, all right."

Sam muttered under his breath. He stopped the wagon and shielded his eyes and studied the distant figure carefully. Hassle had not been mistaken; it was a woman. "Maybe some nestor's wife," the pitchman ventured, "lookin' for livestock."

"I don't see any livestock. I don't see any farms, either."

"Well," the pitchman grumbled, "whoever it is, I reckon she knows what she's doin'." He hollered at the mules and the wagon resumed its jolting way to the southeast. The boy looked at Sam from the corner of his eye but said nothing. If the pitchman wanted to leave a woman afoot on the prairie, there was nothing he could do about it.

They traveled on for several minutes in what was becoming a strained silence. The woman was no longer walking, she was standing quite still, watching the wagon. "If she was in any kind of trouble," Sam said to himself, "she'd wave or somethin'."

The woman didn't wave. She merely stood there, as rigidly erect as a sun-dance pole on the edge of the world. California Sam heaved an angry sigh. "Well, it means we won't make Pond Creek till sometime tomorrow, but I guess there ain't nothin' for it now." With a good deal of profanity he hauled the mules around and headed the wagon toward the standing woman.

The distance was greater than it had appeared at first. "I must be out of my head," the pitchman snarled under his breath, "goin' to all this trouble over a nestor woman."

"It ain't a nestor woman," Hassle told him.

Sam squinted his watery eyes. "Who else would be out walkin' on the prairie? Who is it if it ain't a nestor woman?"

"I think," the boy told him mildly, "it's Miss Rose McGee."

California Sam looked as if he had been hit in the face with a saddle blanket. He rubbed his eyes and stared long and hard at the distant figure. "By God," he said in astonishment, "you're right, boy! It's that thievin'-hearted pennyweighter from the Western Trail Saloon, sure's a toad's got three toes!"

"You reckon she's in trouble?" the youth asked innocently.

California Sam took a deep breath, rubbed his hands together and grinned savagely. "If she ain't," the pitchman promised fervently, "she soon will be!"

Rose McGee watched the approach of the wagon with a curious lack of emotion. She neither feared nor welcomed the appearance of the medicine man. So much had happened to her in the past three days that it didn't seem possible that anything else could hurt her. So she stood there dumbly, one side of her face black with dried blood, her whipcord riding dress soiled and tattered beyond any hope of repair.

There was no doubt in her mind regarding the identity

of that wagon—there could only be one wagon in the world like that one. And she had a very good notion what the medicine man's attitude would be concerning the loss of his valuable diamond stickpin. But none of that mattered to her now, neither the threat of prison nor the likelihood of violence. It simply didn't matter.

As the wagon drew closer Rose experienced the faintest twinge of curiosity at the sight of young Hassle Jones riding on the seat beside the medicine man—but that too passed almost immediately. She was too emotionally and physically exhausted to care about anyone, or anything. She regarded the medicine man's angry, beefsteak-colored face, it did not intimidate her, did not touch her. The worst thing that could happen to a woman had already happened to Rose McGee—her pride in being a woman had been destroyed.

As the wagon rattled toward her, Rose absently brushed her hair out of her eyes. She noticed that her arm was stiff, her shoulder painfully bruised. Her shoes were in tatters and her feet were sore and swollen.

As the distance between the wagon and Rose McGee narrowed, Hassle watched the medicine man with considerable interest. California Sam's face was beet-red. His eyes glittered. "Boy," he snarled at Hassle from the side of his mouth, "this here's goin' to be about the sweetest day in my life! To grab myself a pennyweighter and . . ."

But the words trailed off into a puzzled silence. His anger and indignation, having reached a high pitch, now teetered uncertainly. By now they were close enough to see that the woman was somewhat the worse for wear. The black smear on her face could only be dried blood. The condition of her clothing suggested that she had been unhorsed somewhere up the line. Probably dragged for a considerable distance, with her foot in the stirrup.

With only a few feet now separating them, Sam hauled the mules to a stop and set the brake. Rose McGee looked at him with a bleakness that made his insides shrink. "She's hurt," Hassle said, waiting to see what the medicine man would do.

"Goddammit, boy," Sam snapped at him, "I can see that." He wrapped the lines and cautiously climbed down over the front wheel. He approached her with more caution, worriedly squinting his bloodshot eyes.

From his place on the driver's seat, Hassle found this reunion of saloon woman and medicine man fascinating. At the age of eleven he had got to know many saloon women, but he liked Rose McGee. There had been a robust cheerfulness about her that he had admired. Also, she hadn't considered it beneath her dignity to talk to a boy of eleven. More than once, as Hassle drifted through the Western Trail Saloon looking for odd jobs, Rose had invented useless chores for him so that he could earn a few pennies. Sometimes, in the early part of the day when saloon business was slack, she would let him sit at her table and drink coffee with her. "We're two of a kind, Hassle," she told him once. "Over there on the other side of the fence there's the whole world. Over here on this side there's folks like you and me. All by ourselves."

For several seconds California Sam merely looked at Rose McGee. Then, with a grunt of profound disgust—disgust for what, Hassle wasn't sure—the pitchman pushed back his widebrim beaver and called over his shoulder, "Boy, break out the canteen. And that bottle of Kentucky whiskey." To Rose McGee he said, "How long you been afoot like this?"

She didn't appear to understand him. Her eyes had a curious blankness. "Hurry up with that water, boy!"

Hassle scrambled down over the wheel with the water and whiskey. Rose grasped the canteen in both hands and gulped convulsively, spilling a good deal of the water down the front of her dress. "Now try a little touch of this," Sam told her, handing her the bottle.

Obediently, Rose swigged from the neck of the bottle. Her eyes seemed to clear a little. "Better see if you can clear out a place for her in the wagon," Sam said to his young assistant.

As Hassle scurried away, Rose reached again for the bottle, but the pitchman quickly corked it. "Later. First, let's find out what happened to you. The stablehand at Wichita said you left town on one of his horses. Did you get throwed?"

Rose nodded her head woodenly and said, "Went off a cut bank durin' the night. Broke his neck in the fall, I guess. Dead. I hit my head on an outcrop and . . ." She gestured vaguely. "You're the last person I ever expected to see out here on the prairie."

"I *bet*," Sam told her unpleasantly. "You think you can walk?"

Her eyes seemed to lose their focus. "Sure I can walk. What do you think I've been doin' all this . . ." She took one step and dropped to her knees. With a groan, the pitchman picked her up and carried her to the wagon.

With Hassle's help he got Rose into the wagon and stretched her out between boxes of soap and herbs and salves, fitting her around cans of alcohol and crates of empty medicine bottles and bundles of Wa-Hoe medicine labels. She made no comment and offered no objection. The bleakness had returned to her eyes; she didn't seem to know or care what was happening to her.

California Sam sat on a box of "chopped grass"—mixed herbs—and looked at her for several seconds. To Hassle's amazement, he did not once mention the diamond stickpin. At last he said, "We got to be goin' now. When we find a place we'll make camp for the night, but until then you'll have to make out here in the back of the wagon. You goin' to be all right?"

She regarded him with amazement of her own. "Is that all you got to say? After what I did to you?"

"Time for that later; I ain't forgettin'. You want another touch of this whiskey?"

She shook her head. "No, not now."

"Well . . ." The pitchman heaved himself off the box of herbs. "If the goin' gets too rough back here, give a holler and I'll try to find a smoother track."

Sam returned to the driver's seat and once again headed the mules in the general direction of Pond Creek. Hassle said worriedly, "She don't look so good to me. Is she bad hurt?"

The pitchman shrugged. "I don't think so. But sometimes it's hard to tell about women." There was a strange look on the boy's face. Sam said, "You're not lookin' so good yourself. You're not ailin', are you?"

Hassle shook his head. "I guess I was just wonderin' about things. I was expectin' you to lay into Rose good about that stickpin."

"Time for everything, boy," Sam told him grimly. "Everything in its time."

5

CROY MEEKER was digging postholes on the southwest quarter of his claim when the horsebacker came riding toward him from the east. Croy wiped his sweaty face and regarded the stranger with mild curiosity. "Howdy," he said, eying the filthy bandanna that covered the horsebacker's head.

"Is that water fit to drink?" the stranger demanded, indicating a small stream that ran through Meeker's quarter section. Meeker told him it was a sweetwater stream, so the stranger got down and led his horse to the stream. They drank together, man and animal, at the edge of the water.

"How far to Pond Creek?" the stranger asked.

There was something about the man that rankled Meeker. He didn't ask questions, he demanded answers. But Meeker was a peaceful man and he merely shrugged. "Maybe twenty miles, if you follow the crow. Some farther if you take the mail road."

Dutch Rainey got down on his knees and splashed water over his head. Very carefully, he peeled the blood-spotted bandanna off of his head and rinsed it in the stream. Meeker was startled at the condition of the man's scalp. The skin was dried and cracked like an old saddle that had lain too long in the weather. The stranger's blond beard and fair complexion would explain a certain sensitiveness to the elements, but this was the first time Meeker had ever seen a man's whole scalp curl up and crack like a green hide in the sun.

"Mister," Croy Meeker started politely, "if you don't mind me askin' . . ."

Dutch whirled on him, his eyes burning. "It happens I do mind."

The farmer shrugged. "Well, all right. Help yourself to the water." He picked up his posthole digger and returned to work. But between postholes he could not help wondering what had happened to the man's scalp.

And there was another thing that disturbed Meeker—the condition of the stranger's horse. The animal was obviously on the verge of collapse. It stood hip-shot, head hanging, beside the water. Croy Meeker had not always been a farmer; he had once been a cowhand and knew horses. He didn't like to see animals mistreated the way this sorrel had been mistreated.

After a moment of consideration, Meeker rested on his posthole digger and made a suggestion. "Why don't you unbit, maybe throw off the saddle for a spell, and rest that sorrel?"

Dutch Rainey replaced the wet bandanna and tied it in place around his head. "Why don't you keep your notions to yourself? I don't want to hear them."

"Just tryin' to help," the farmer shrugged. He returned to digging postholes.

Dutch drank some more water and then sat for a while beside the stream and smoked a cigarette. His face was gray with exhaustion, but the fire of hatred was in his eyes. Hatred, and shattered pride, and general frustration. The subject of California Sam, the medicine man, had become an obsession with him. He couldn't make himself close his eyes and sleep. He couldn't eat or rest or focus his mind on anything but that pitchman. "I'm lookin' for a man," he said at last to the farmer. "A horse-faced galoot wearin' buckskin pants and coat. A medicine show doc."

Croy Meeker shook his head. "I don't recollect seein' anybody like that."

"He travels in a wagon that's painted all over with pictures," Dutch continued, "pulled by a team of gray mules. He left Wichita three days ago and most likely is headin' for Pond Creek. He must of come this way."

Meeker thought it over carefully. As a matter of fact he had seen such a wagon, but he hesitated to mention it. There was violence in this stranger's face—maybe even murder. Croy didn't want anything to do with that.

Still, it was not easy to deny a man obsessed. As the stranger studied him closely, the farmer began to sweat. Dutch got to his feet and walked toward Meeker, his hand resting on the butt of his .45. "You're lyin'," he said quietly. "You seen that pitchman. Or anyway the wagon."

The farmer licked his suddenly dry lips. "Like I just told you, mister, I never saw this medicine show doc."

"The wagon then."

Croy hesitated for a moment, then made his decision. "I never saw the wagon neither."

The decision, as it worked out, was a serious mistake. Without a word, Dutch drew his heavy .45 and slashed the farmer across the face with the barrel. Meeker, his face suddenly numb and bloody, dropped to his knees. He was stunned and frightened. There was madness in the stranger's eyes.

"Think about it some more," Dutch told him coldly. "You right sure you never laid eyes on that wagon?"

The farmer, down on all fours, spat blood and a few front teeth into the brown grass. "Late yesterday," he said at last. "The medicine man and a young boy made camp here. They pulled out this mornin' headin' toward Pond Creek."

Dutch grinned down at him. "See? That wasn't so hard, was it?"

California Sam climbed a small knoll near their campsite and gazed uneasily back to the northeast. For two days now this sense of uneasiness had been nagging him. He couldn't isolate it or define it, but it was there and he respected it. Pitchmen, if they lasted long in their profession, developed a high sensitivity to danger, and Sam had never felt it stronger than he did now. Somewhere along his backtrail there was an outraged yokel with a sore head, or maybe even an unsatisfied user of Wa-Hoe Miracle Soap. There was violence and danger there in the gathering dusk—he could taste it in the dusty air, the way a coyote could taste poisoned bait.

"What I got to do," he told himself, "is get off this prairie and into a town. The bigger the town the better."

The city was the pitchman's natural home. There, in the midst of big buildings and noisy traffic and bustling crowds, he felt secure. But here on the prairie, with the aching silence disturbed only by a rustling of a prairie chicken or a coyote's bark, he was helpless. A pitchman was good at only one thing—the use of words—and on the prairie there were very few people to listen to what a worried medicine man had to say.

Well, he thought, tomorrow they would make Pond Creek. Not a city, maybe, but a good deal better than the wilderness.

In the meantime, there was Rose McGee to think about.

He returned to the wagon where Rose was sitting hunched over on a fallen cottonwood, staring blankly into the fire where Hassle was cooking supper. "How you feelin'?" the pitchman asked.

Rose shrugged. "All right, considerin'. Is there any more of that whiskey left?"

Sam brought out the bottle. He poured some for Rose in a tin cup and the rest for himself. They drank in silence. The only sound was the sputtering of fat meat in Hassle's skillet.

Then, without warning, Rose McGee lurched to her feet and hurled her whiskey to the ground. "Damn you, pitchman!" she hollered at Sam. "Haven't you got any gall at all? Are you goin' to just stand there and cluck like a settin' hen? Ain't you ever goin' to bring up the subject of the watch and money and ring and diamond stickpin that I stole from you?"

"I been thinkin' about it," Sam confessed, only slightly surprised at her outburst. "The way I see it," he went on calmly, "you'll get around to tellin' me sometime. Maybe you'd rather wait till after supper."

"I'd rather do it right now!" she sneered. "Then if you want to turn me out of camp . . ." She shrugged extravagantly. "Well, that's all right with me."

Sam sat down on the cottonwood, filled his corncob pipe and lit it. Rose found his air of imperturbability maddening. She clinched her fists and glared at him, aching to scream. But she made herself sit quietly until she was sure that she could speak in an even tone. "It's gone," she said at last. "It's all gone. The watch I sold for four dollars. The ring," she sneered, "was glass. I sold it for a dollar. The stickpin—it was a real diamond, I guess—I sold for seventy-five dollars."

The pitchman came off the cottonwood as if he had been jabbed with a war lance. "Seventy-five dollars! That diamond was worth seven hundred dollars if it was worth a cent!"

"Seventy-five dollars," she told him again, unmoved. "Watch, ring, stickpin. Eighty dollars in all."

California Sam's face was startlingly pale. Seventy-five dollars! He considered it a personal insult. That beautiful, many-faceted stone adorning the silk (probably imitation silk) cravat of some cheap Wichita gambler—it was almost more than an old pitchman could bear.

He took a long, deep breath and said in a slightly quivering voice, "I don't guess there's any use askin' if you've still got the eighty dollars?"

"Not a penny," she told him belligerently. "Your eighty dollars, along with more'n a hundred dollars of my own—all gone."

"If it won't put you out too much," the pitchman told her, his tone acid and bitter, "I'd be right proud to know where my eighty dollars went."

She slumped again and stared into the fire. When Sam had about decided that she wasn't going to answer him, she said, "Alf got it."

The medicine man looked blank. "Alf?"

"My man, Alf. Alf Ritter." She lifted her head and faced Sam with a dazzling smile. Then, to the pitchman's consternation, he watched two large fat tears form in her eyes and slide like greased bullets along the side of her nose. She lurched up from the log, and after several meaningless sounds and ineffectual gestures, wheeled and raced toward the dark brush where the mules were grazing.

Young Hassle Jones, bent over his cookfire, stared at the pitchman with bugging eyes. Sam shrugged and heaved a sigh. "Women," he said, by way of explanation.

When Rose returned to the fire her eyes were clear and her voice calm. "Was that stickpin really worth seven hundred dollars?" she asked.

"Never mind the stickpin right now, I'd rather hear about Alf."

She nodded. "I guess you've got a right. Well, Alf was a cowhand. He worked in the shippin' pens at Wichita, that's where I got to know him. Alf and me . . . We was goin' to get married."

Sam was already beginning to wish that he hadn't asked. It was an old story—so old that it made him wonder how an experienced saloon woman like Rose McGee could have been taken in by it. But, as he had earlier indicated to Hassle, there was no explaining women.

Rose—as her story had it—had been a woman with a vision. Maybe she had even been in love with Alf—but the vision was the main thing. In this vision she had seen herself—Rose McGee—not as a saloon woman but as plain housewife. A farm wife, with a house of her own—no matter if it was a half dugout with a sod room and dirt floor. A yard with chickens, and children, and maybe a cow. A husband working the fields where she could watch him. In her vision that husband had been Alf Ritter.

From this point her story became vague. Alf had traveled to the newly opened Cherokee Outlet—he had written Rose that he had found the right piece of land; the owner was willing to sell for a cash payment of two hundred dollars. At this point Rose paused in her story to look at California Sam. "I had some over a hundred dollars of my own. Your eighty made up the rest."

Sam decided not to dwell too long on the aspect of her tale. A pitchman, if he was to survive, learned to be a philosopher about some things. "Why didn't you mail him the money?"

She shrugged. After all those years of waiting, she wanted to see that vision of hers with her own eyes.

From this point on the story became painful to listen to. She met Alf at a crossroads store in the Outlet and gave him the two hundred dollars to arrange the purchase of the land. Alf—the pitchman could see him, cheerful, grinning, with a face full of yellow teeth—assured her that everything would be settled before nightfall. Rose, at Alf's insistence, was to wait at the store.

Rose waited.

She waited all that day and into the night. At last she had borrowed quilts for a pallet and spent the night with the storekeeper's family. There had been some small difficulty about the land purchase, she told herself. Alf was sure to show up the next day.

He did not show up. Rose waited through the second night. Something inside her seemed to die. The next morning she thanked the storekeeper and his wife for their kindness and she rode away.

She smiled vaguely at Sam and Hassle. "Well, that horse I got from the wagon yard at Wichita wasn't much of a horse. He went off a cut bank. Went right off and broke his neck clean as you please. Damn' near broke mine, too—for a while I wished I had. Well," she sighed with a brilliant fake smile, "that's the way it was. That's what happened to your things that I stole. Alf's got the money. And I guess Alf's a long way from here by this time."

Sam couldn't think of anything to say. They sat in uncomfortable silence for a while, then Hassle dished up the hoecake and side meat and canned tomatoes and they ate supper.

"I'm out of whiskey," Sam told Rose later. "There's some alcohol that I mix my herbs with, if you don't mind it bein' a little green."

She shook her head. After a while she said, "You don't have to do this, you know."

"Do what?"

"Take me in like this. You don't owe me anything."

"I know. But I owe it to myself to keep you alive till I get back the price of my stickpin."

"If you don't mind me askin', just how do you manage to do that?"

"That," the pitchman told her grimly, "is somethin' I ain't quite got figgered out yet. But I will."

They let the subject of the stickpin drop—it was painful to both of them. Sam wandered off to look after the mules, and Rose helped Hassle wash the dishes. The pitchman stood for a while, just beyond the flickering rim of firelight, and watched them. Saloon woman and young boy, they were chattering like ground squirrels. Once, to California Sam's amazement, he heard Hassle laugh. It occurred to him that he had never heard the boy laugh before.

That night Rose slept in the wagon and the pitchman slept on the ground, which did not improve his temper the next morning. He got up stiff and sore, snarling at Hassle, the mules, and Rose McGee. He complained that the coffee was gritty, the bacon overcooked, the panbread burned. But it wasn't really the food that bothered him, it wasn't even the inconvenience of having a woman in camp and being forced to sleep on the ground. There was an electricity in the air that raised the short hairs on his neck and made his skin prickle. Whether it was actually the weather, or whether it was his overactive sense of impending danger, he could not definitely say.

"Goddammit, boy!" he brayed at Hassle. "Put some dirt on that fire! Can't you see the prairie's dry as gunpowder?"

"You can't boil coffee without a fire," the youth told him aloofly.

"Then let the coffee go. It's time we started travelin' anyhow."

It was quietly understood that Rose would get herself a saloon job in Pond Creek, if she didn't return to Wichita, and that would be the last they would see of her. They struck again toward the southwest, away from the fiercely burning July sun. For the second day running a hot wind came up in the east, bending and rustling the prairie grass. Every few minutes the pitchman would turn and look nervously back over his shoulder. What he was looking for he didn't know.

Toward midmorning Dutch Rainey topped a grassy rise—and there it was. The wagon.

Dutch stood in his stirrups and grinned fiercely when he saw it. There was no doubt about it; there it was, about a mile to the east, crawling like a small, gaudy bug over the brown curve of the prairie.

Dutch, with the true instincts of a killer, drew his saddle rifle from the boot and aimed it at that distant speck on the prairie. The range was much too great to risk a shot, but it gave him pleasure simply to watch the wagon over the sights.

"Just me and you, Doc," he said aloud, "all by ourselves here in the middle of nowhere. It won't be long now!"

Impatiently, he raked the staggering sorrel with his spurs. The animal stumbled crazily for perhaps a hundred yards. Then, to Dutch's savage cursing, the sorrel fell to its knees, somersaulted head over heels, flinging its rider to the hard sod.

For several minutes Dutch lay gasping, his right foot still in the stirrup. The horse lay wheezing raggedly, watching him with hurt, sick eyes. Dutch knew that the sorrel was finished. The animal was as good as dead. Very carefully, the rider shoved himself to a sitting position and pulled his foot out of the stirrup. There was a long needle of pain in his leg; his knee was beginning to puff like a hog bladder in the sun. For several anxious moments he inspected the injured limb. It was not broken, he decided, but the knee was badly twisted.

Walking, for any considerable distance, was out of the question. And the sorrel lay dying.

For perhaps ten minutes Dutch Rainey lay clutching his knee, his brain on fire with rage and frustration. He crawled to his rifle and aimed the weapon at the wagon—but the pitchman was far beyond the range of any saddlegun. Even as he watched, the wagon moved farther away. Soon it would be out of sight, out of his reach—maybe forever.

Then, slowly and quietly, a new hope began to take shape in Dutch's brain. Somewhere in the fire and rage a small thought, as hard as stone, survived. Dutch made himself be calm. With a mother's love he nursed that small germ of an idea, and it began to grow.

And it grew. And after a while there it was, full-grown, shimmering, and deadly.

Dutch put down the rifle and moved his band of his hat. He was gleefully and savagely aware of the hot, dry wind blowing from the east. He took a sulphur match from the hatband. He struck the match and dropped it into the dry, brown grass.

California Sam was idly wondering if there was a wholesale drug outfit in Pond Creek where he could replenish his supply of herbs, when the whole prairie seemed to explode.

Rose McGee, riding beside the pitchman on the driver's seat, jumped at the sound of distant thunder. But it was not thunder. Sam quickly turned and looked back over his shoulder, as he had done so many times before—and this time he was not disappointed. Death and destruction, in the form of boiling smoke and dancing fangs of flame, was riding the wind, hurtling toward them.

Young Hassle Jones, dozing in the back of the wagon, stuck his head through the puckered opening and demanded, "What's that noise?"

"Prairie fire," the pitchman said softly, almost to himself. "Heavens help us all!" In the vocabulary of the plainsman no words were more fearsome. Neither "plague" nor "drought," nor "blizzard" nor "Cyclone." Nothing quite produced the terror of "prairie fire!"

Rose stared wide-eyed at the black, boiling monster that was devouring the prairie. "Grab hold of somethin'," Sam told her. "Looks like we got some hard travelin' ahead." He twisted his head and glanced at Hassle. "You too, boy. Keep an eye on my herbs and that can of alcohol." He hollered at the mules, and the wagon lurched across the open prairie.

The mules' ears lay back flat against their heads. Their eyes rolled wildly in their sockets. They had smelled the smoke and all their instincts told them that it was the smell of fiery death. There was no need for the pitchman to call on the whip; the animals were racing ahead of the fire with all the strength and speed that had been bred into them.

And they were losing ground by the second. The grasping arms of the fire stretched as far as the eye could see. It ran with the sound of thunder, moving at almost unbelievable speed.

"Make the mules go faster!" Hassle hollered from the back of the wagon. "It's gainin' on us!"

"Settle down," the pitchman told him with calmness that he did not feel. "I think I see some timber up ahead. A creek, most likely. We'll be safe there."

But there was no timber there, and no creek, it was just something to say.

Then, from out of nowhere, a flight of doves appeared—in their frantic flight from the fire they smashed themselves against the side of the wagon. Rose McGee stared in terror at the bloody spot on the painted canvas. A rabbit streaked across the path of the pounding mules and was immediately trampled into the dusty sod. A white-tailed deer passed the wagon with less than a yard to spare and continued on its twisting, panic-stricken way. Where had that deer been hiding all this time, on the open prairie? Sam shook his head in wonder.

As if by magic the sky was suddenly dark with terrified birds. With screaming larks and doves and prairie chickens and plovers. With awkward turkeys beating the air with their heavy wings. With graceful scissortails and thrushes.

A startling gathering of animals materialized in the brown grass—coyotes racing shoulder to shoulder with prairie wolves and rabbits. Ancient milk cows and tired old work horses raced like gazelles, their blood hot with terror. Prairie dogs and ground squirrels ran with rattlesnakes and streaking black racers, comrades in fear now, brothers in blind panic.

Sam shot another look over his shoulder and was appalled to see how rapidly the fire was gaining. Not improving the situation, the mules were tiring. They were beginning to stumble in the heavy grass. If one of them went down—Sam forced himself to consider the possibility—if one of the mules went down, that would end it. The fire would overtake them in a matter of minutes.

It was then that the pitchman realized that they did not stand the slightest chance of outrunning the fire. At the rate it was now spreading, it would overtake them in a matter of ten or fifteen minutes. Much sooner, if the mules gave out.

In some mysterious way his thoughts became calm and orderly. For some minutes he sat beside Rose McGee on the seat of the lurching wagon, his long, unhandsome face quietly thoughtful. He no longer regarded the fire as a fire, but as "the enemy." He thought of it as a mob of angry yokels coming after him with hot tar and chicken feathers. One thing he had learned from his years as a pitchman: never let a sucker see that he had you buffaloed. The louder he hollered and the more threats he made, the more self-assured a pitchman became. Because, if he was a real pitchman, his brain would be working with the speed and precision of a railroad conductor's silver-plated watch.

Of course, the practice of thinking, like anything else, could be overdone. It was entirely possible for a pitchman to become so absorbed in his own cleverness that he found himself on his way out of town straddling a rail.

With something like a sigh of resignation, Sam suddenly

stood on the brake and began hauling on the lines. Rose McGee stared appalled as the mules came to a stumbling halt. "Are you out of your head? What do you think you're doin'?"

California Sam thrust the lines into her hands. "Hold the team. Boy," he shouted to Hassle, "get up here and help her."

Open-mouthed, the youth climbed over the back of the seat and helped Rose hold the frightened mules. Before they had time to make further objections, the pitchman climbed down to the ground and began running away from the wagon. When he was about a hundred yards from the wagon he stopped, fumbled in his pockets for a moment and glanced back at Rose and Hassle. To their amazement, he grinned. It was weak and watered down and a little on the sickish side, but still a grin.

A rattlesnake brushed against the pitchman's legs in its headlong flight from the fire. A wild-eyed coyote almost ran over him as he stood there, dangling for that last second on the thread of indecision. Then, with his big jaw jutting in determination, the medicine man took out a match, struck it and dropped it into the grass.

Horrified, Rose and Hassle witnessed his crime. Almost instantly a wall of fire leapt up. Sam sprinted fifty paces to his right and started another fire. Within three minutes he had five fires going, each spreading with appalling speed. He saw the rattlesnake thrashing helplessly as the fire overtook it. Lord help me, he thought, with a hard, sick ball in the pit of his stomach. I've done some things in my time that I'm not right proud of, but nothin' like this.

But when he returned to the wagon his face was blank with unconcern. With an air of indifference he regarded the faces of Rose and Hassle. "It's our only chance," he told them. "Burn off a spot and move into it before the main fire reaches us."

They looked at him as if he had just slaughtered, with his own hands, a whole settlement of women and children.

For a time it seemed inevitable that they would be caught between the two gigantic walls of fire. Between the two racing fires boiled a canopy of dirty black smoke from which fell a fiery rain of live sparks. The two mules began to rear in panic. Sam jerked off his fancy buckskin jacket and tried to cover their heads. But they were too filled with fear now; they were beyond control.

The pitchman hesitated only a moment. For just a second he paused and regarded the wagon, as a mother might regard an only child. Then his face turned curiously blank. "Boy," he shouted to Hassle, "get down there and help me unhitch these mules."

"What about the wagon?" the practical young Hassle Jones demanded.

"The wagon's gone, boy. Done for. I don't see much sense in lettin' the mules go with it."

They released the mules, and the two animals raced in blind panic through a wall of smoke. A rabbit ran into Sam's legs and, savage as a lion, bit the medicine man's ankle.

"Get the wagon canteen," Sam hollered to Rose McGee. "See if you can find a rag of some kind. Wet it and wrap it around your head."

Rose, dimly beginning to understand that perhaps the medicine man was not quite mad after all, quickly tore off a strip of petticoat, soaked it with water from the canteen and handed half to Hassle.

"Godamighty!" Sam bellowed, as his head began to tingle. He jerked off his beaver hat and quickly beat out a fire in the crown.

Rose poured some water in his hat and handed him the canteen. "Ain't there anything we can do about the wagon?" she asked. "Couldn't the three of us pull it to a place that's already burned out?"

"The only thing you can do about the wagon is put it

out of your mind," Sam told her. "It's done for. So'll we be if we don't get away from here."

She turned in alarm and saw that the wagon's canvas cover was already burning. The sky was raining fire; their clothing was smoking in a dozen places. Sam and Hassle handed her down from the driver's seat an instant before the wagon exploded in violent blue flame.

"My alcohol!" the pitchman groaned. They stood in dumb fascination watching the wagon burn. For a few seconds the fiery air was fragrant with senna and sassafras and berberis and anis. Then another can of alcohol exploded. A case of medicine bottles went off like a volley of rifles. Almost before they knew it the wagon was reduced to a heap of charred wood and ashes. And then, with breathtaking suddenness, the prairie fire was upon them.

It arrived with the sound of a howling storm. "Everybody stay close together!" Sam hollered. The three of them raced across the stretch of unburned grass that lay between the wagon and the fire that Sam had set. The set fire lay somewhere ahead of them, ahead of a rolling wall of dirty smoke. Rose hesitated at the edge of that blackened, smoke-filled world which was their only hope for survival. The charred earth seemed to be alive. Bright snakes of fire crawled along the ground. More fire fell out of the sky.

"I can't go in there!" Rose said, shaking her head. "I just can't."

"Ma'am," Sam told her coldly, "this ain't no time for foolishness." He grasped her hand and pulled into the world of swirling smoke and raining fire. Rose and Hassle wrapped the wet strips of petticoat around their heads; Sam buried his face in his dampened hat. They stumbled ahead blindly, with the great roar of the fire at their backs.

"This is far enough," Sam said at last. They huddled together as the fire angrily probed for a way through the already burned grass. It seemed to roar it's frustration. It spewed fire and sparks on their hunched backs. Rose and

Hassle began coughing, and Sam poured some water over their heads. He poured more water into his hat, but nothing seemed to help now. Tears streamed from their eyes. They fell into another fit of coughing. The heat was searing. All the air had been sucked into the ravenous belly of the fire; their small sanctuary was now a roaring vacuum in which there was only smoke and more smoke.

Then, like a maddened animal racing up and down the borders of their burned-out world, the fire suddenly streaked to the north and was gone.

How long it had lasted, they didn't know. Miraculously, the wind freshened and swept away most of the smoke. They stood like three charred stumps in the middle of a burned-out forest, coughing, gasping, endless tears streaming down their black faces.

The pitchman beat out a small fire on Rose McGee's dress. They drank some water from the canteen, and washed their eyes and wiped their faces. Little by little they stopped their coughing. Their tears plowed more dirty furrows down their sooty faces, but after a time the tears stopped too. They stared at one another, amazed at being alive. Finally they looked with reddened eyes at the prairie where the fire had fed.

Rose McGee made a small whimpering sound. The prairie, as far as they could see in any direction, was black and smoking. Here and there, in heavy clumps of buffalo grass, tongues of red still flickered. The main fire had raced on out of sight, leaving behind it great clouds of smoke rolling and tumbling like enormous thunderheads.

The pitchman abstractedly began patting his chest, feeling for pockets that were not there. He groaned to himself —a great, heartfelt sound of disgust. "Somewheres along the line I lost my coat. When we was unhitchin' the mules, I guess."

Rose and Hassle looked at him in amazement. With the wagon and team lost, the whole prairie burned, thousands of animals killed, millions of dollars worth of grass destroyed—the pitchman worried about his fancy buckskin coat.

He saw what they were thinking, but at the moment he didn't feel like explaining that all his money had been in that coat. He had known disaster before, and he knew that no matter how bad a situation looked at first glance, a little money was always a comfort. Well, he thought, maybe it was better they didn't think about it right now.

"Lord knows," he sighed, gazing up at the empty sky, "where we're at. Or when we'll see signs of life again." The sky was empty of birds, and no animal stirred on that black and smoking plain. "Well," he added with fake cheerfulness, "we might as well start walkin'."

Rose looked down at her shoes which were smoking and half burned off her feet. Then she looked at the pitchman and smiled a smile so bleak and cheerless that California Sam's singed hair seemed to rise on the back of his neck. "You and the boy go on," she said. "I don't feel like walkin' right now; maybe I'll catch up later."

Sam squinted his bloodshot eyes and looked at her closely. He found it hard to believe that this was the woman with the brassbound gall to steal the last cent from a high pitchman. Her spirit was gone. The last spark had gone up in fire and smoke. Well, the medicine man quietly decided, that last thing she needs right now is pity; she's gettin' plenty of that from herself.

Aloud he said, "Just what do you aim to do? Set down and give up the ghost, like an old wore-out Comanche warrior?"

She smiled that smile again. "I'm just tired, I guess."

Sam shrugged indifferently. "Well, it's your business, you can handle it any way that suits you. Boy," he said to Hassle, "you ready to start walkin'?"

The youth looked at the medicine man and scowled fiercely. "You can't just walk off and leave her!"

"I can do anything that suits me, son. And what suits me right now is some walkin'." He glanced up at the sun to get his bearings, then began striding off to the west.

The boy took Rose's arm and gave it an anxious tug. "He means it, ma'am. He'll walk off and leave us."

Rose tried to free herself from his grip. "You go on, Hassle. I want to be by myself for a while."

Hassle glared his stern disapproval. "It won't do no good ma'am. It won't bring back that man of yours. And it won't bring back the two hundred dollars you gave him. If I was you I'd put him out of my head and stick to California Sam."

She smiled fleetingly. "You ain't me, Hassle. Anyway, stickin' to the medicine man don't seem like such a smart thing to me. You've been stickin' to him, and now look at yourself."

Hassle was unimpressed with her argument. "I know things don't look so good right now, but I knowed worse times."

She looked at him in surprise. "You like that pitchman, don't you?"

"Like him?" The boy sneered at the word, as if liking someone had to be a sure sign of weakness. "I don't feel one way or the other about him. But he saved us from the fire, didn't he? I reckon if we stick with him he'll show us the way to that railroad town."

"Then you go with him, Hassle."

"No ma'am." The youth stuck his jaw out stubbornly. "I wouldn't do a thing like that. I don't go unless you go."

"Then we'll both stay."

"All right, we'll stay."

Rose McGee lifted her chin and gazed resolutely at the dark horizon. Some hundred yards away California Sam was plowing through the ocean of black grass. His stride was brisk and charged with confidence—or arrogance—and he did not once look back at his two companions.

"I just thought of somethin'," Hassle said nervously.

"Thought of what?"

"He's got the canteen. It's goin' to get mighty thirsty here in the middle of a burned prairie without no water."

Rose McGee lifted her chin a little higher and said nothing.

"You're lucky," Hassle told her with waning patience, "and just ain't got the sense to know it."

She glared down at him. "Lucky?"

"What if you'd *married* that Alf Ritter? Then you'd *really* have somethin' to be long-faced about!"

After walking for an hour the pitchman paused to get his breath and take a pull on the canteen. He glanced back over his shoulder and was not surprised to see Hassle and the saloon woman following his wake at a lively clip. Good, he thought to himself. Keep the pace fast enough and they won't have so much time to worry about things that ain't important.

Sometime that afternoon he raised a stand of blackened cottonwoods and began to breathe a little easier. He stood for a moment looking at the reddish water of a small creek. On the far side of the stream the grass was summer brown, not black. Evidently the fire, instead of jumping the water, had streaked north. With luck, it would eventually turn on itself, scorpion-like, and burn itself to death.

Kneeling beside the stream, Sam filled his hat with water and poured it over his head. He sat for a long while wishing that he hadn't lost his pipe and tobacco. Slowly, he began unbuttoning his shirt. He stripped off his shirt, his charred buckskin pants, his tattered button shoes. Finally he peeled off his union suit and got into the water.

He sank into the tepid water with the groaning luxury of a *Police Gazette* beauty queen bathing in a tub of champagne. Sitting on the muddy bottom, in water to his chin, he thought aloud, "I'd give ten dollars cash for one bar of Wa-Hoe Miracle Soap right now!"

When Hassle and Rose McGee stumbled down the long grade to the creek, the medicine man was still in the water, energetically beating his soot-blackened clothing with a cottonwood stick. Young Hassle Jones looked at him and grinned. Somehow, the picture of a high pitchman, naked as a jaybird, sitting in the middle of a creek washing clothes, struck him as funny.

Rose McGee did not find it funny or even interesting. She sank to her knees and splashed the clay-tinted water on her face, then she lay back against a stump and seemed to fall asleep.

California Sam glared beneath his shaggy brows at Hassle and gathered his dignity about him like an invisible cloak. "Boy, my advice to you is to stop grinnin' like a possum and wash yourself off in this creek. It's apt to be the last water you'll see between here and the railroad."

Hassle shrugged, his face as black as the prairie itself. He had an eleven-year-old boy's instinctive dislike for water, except as used occasionally for drinking purposes. "I'll wait. Most likely I'll have to wash when I get to Pond Creek anyhow."

"You'll wash now," the pitchman told him coolly, "if you aim to travel with me." He turned and fixed his gaze on Rose McGee. "That goes for you, too, ma'am. When a high pitchman comes into a town he does it with style. That holds for the folks that are with him—if he happens to be foolish enough to be travelin' with company."

The saloon woman opened her eyes and regarded him with distaste. It was clearly in her mind to tell him in the colorful language of Omar's Western Trail exactly what he could do with his superior airs and fetish for bathing. But, on further reflection, she decided against it. For one thing, she began to realize that she was every bit as filthy as Hassle and the medicine man. For another, she strongly suspected that he wouldn't hesitate to walk off and leave her where she sat if she failed to act on his suggestion.

Upstream from Sam and Hassle, behind a convenient thicket of redbud bushes, Rose took off her dress which was hardly any longer recognizable as a piece of wearing apparel. She threw it in the water. Quickly, she skinned out of her petticoats, her undervest and drawers, and waded into midstream. She sank into the warm water and let it wash the grime and the smell of smoke from her body. Downstream, young Hassle Jones complained bitterly. California Sam muttered dire threats and continued to beat his clothing with the cottonwood stick.

Rose McGee heard none of it. Her mind was as pleasantly blank as her life—until the past few days—had been. She didn't even think about Alf Ritter. She rubbed her body with sand until it glowed. She followed the medicine man's example and cleaned her clothes by beating them with a stick. For a time she created a world of her own in which there were no saloons, no men like Alf Ritter—only the warm, soothing water.

Gradually she became aware of the voices from the lower part of the stream. Something had happened; the pitchman's voice was suddenly hot and angry. "Goddammit, boy, I asked you a question and I want an answer!"

"And I told you!" Hassle replied, fiercely resentful as only an eleven-year-old boy could be. "It ain't none of your business!"

"I'm makin' it my business. When a body travels with me I got a right to know somethin' about him."

"Don't let it bother you," the boy shot back. "I won't be travelin' with you any more. I can look after myself."

Quickly, Rose waded to the bank, got into her wet clothing and called, "What's goin' on down there?"

A sudden indignant and angry silence answered her. Muttering to herself, she pulled on her stockings, buttoned her charred, red-top shoes, and went to see for herself what the commotion was about.

The medicine man was standing on the bank in his freshly washed buckskins. Hassle was still in the water, but angrily pulling on his tattered blue shirt. Rose looked at the two of them and tasted electricity in the air. "What's all the hollerin' about?" she demanded.

"You better ask the boy," Sam told her.

The saloon woman moved to the edge of the water. "Hassle? What is it?"

The boy shrugged with elaborate indifference. "It ain't nothin'. He just likes to holler."

"Take off your shirt," the pitchman said. "Let her see for herself."

Rose scowled. "See what?"

"The whipmarks on his back."

"They ain't whipmarks!" the boy retorted angrily. "It was a switch, there never was no whip!" Somehow this had become a point of honor with him—the dozen or so long, poorly healed scars on his back, had *not* been made by a whip. "A peachtree switch," he said again, his chin high. "That's all it was."

The saloon woman's sand-scrubbed face had gone strangely pale. "Let me see, Hassle."

"No. Anyhow, there ain't anything to look at."

"Turn around."

Hassle folded his arms and set his jaw. But Rose's hot gaze locked with his and would not let him go. As last the boy moved his thin shoulders in a shrug of elaborate indifference. "Hell's afire! I keep sayin' there ain't nothin' to see!"

"Don't swear. Now turn around."

Reluctantly, the boy turned. For one long minute Rose studied the whitish scars across his back. "Who did it?"

"That's what I wanted to know," Sam told her, "when he started all that fuss."

Hassle glared and quickly buttoned his shirt. "It wasn't *me* makin' the fuss."

"Who did it?" Rose asked again. "Somebody at the wagon yard where you slept?"

"No."

"Somebody else in Wichita, then?"

Hassle shook his head with an air of infinite boredom. "No."

"Then somebody before you came to Wichita?"

California Sam made a sound deep in his throat. "Maybe that uncle of yours back in Missouri. Is that the reason you ran away?"

The boy hesitated for several seconds and then gave another of his highly complicated shrugs. "What if it is? It's over and done with now. I forgot all about it." Then, for a moment, he fixed the pitchman with a still, calculating gaze and said, "You're not goin' to send me back. If that's what you're thinkin', you can just put it out of your head!"

Sam took a deep breath and let it out with a slow whistle. "That," he said quietly, "ain't what I was thinkin'. Now get out of the water. We got us some walkin' to do."

6

DUTCH RAINEY was a happy man. In spite of the lost sorrel and a painfully twisted knee, he was filled with a hugely satisfying sense of accomplishment. As far as his pale eyes could see, the prairie lay in smoking waste. The spot where the medicine man's wagon had been was now only another charred spot on an enormously charred prairie. There was no sign of the pitchman. There was not even any sign of the team. Everything had been wiped out by the fire. Like a giant avenging hand, he thought with a wide grin, wiping the prairie clean.

For most of the afternoon Dutch sat on a small knoll, a short distance back from the point where he had started the fire, nursing his throbbing knee and admiring his handiwork. Somewhere out there—he couldn't say exactly where—lay the pitchman, as black and charred as the prairie itself. If it hadn't been for his aching knee he would have walked the mile or so into that black wasteland just to see what a burned medicine show pitchman looked like. But that was not important now. The important thing was the medicine man was dead.

At last, when it became clear that there was no more satisfaction to be had from staring at that black, dead expanse of charred grass, Dutch Rainey cut himself a makeshift crutch from a thornbush and began hobbling back toward the east.

Earlier in the day several homesteaders and cowmen had gathered on a higher knoll behind the one where Dutch sat, to watch the fire. Maybe to watch their crops and cattle go up in rolling clouds of smoke. Most of them had left the place by midafternoon, but there was still one man with a team and wagon.

Leaning heavily on his crutch, Dutch made his way up the long grade to the top of the knoll. "Howdy," he said cheerfully to the sodbuster. "I lost my saddle animal over there on the next rise. Got my knee twisted some. I'd be much obliged if I could ride along with you to the next settlement."

The man looked at him blankly. "Did you see how the fire started?"

"Just started," Dutch shrugged. "The prairie does that sometime, in the summer. You're not from around these parts?"

"Colorado," the farmer said dully. "Moved my family down last year when they opened the Outlet. Put a piece of bottom land in cotton and corn. There it is . . ." He pointed to the blackened wasteland. "Out there somewheres. I don't reckon you happened to see anything of a woman and boy, did you? The boy'll be four years old come September."

Dutch shook his head. "Never seen anybody at all, just some livestock. You got a house out there?"

"A dugout," the man said in a curiously flat voice. "I aimed to start a better house soon's the crop's in. But for now we're livin' in a dugout."

"You're lucky," Dutch told him, rubbing his throbbing knee. "Not even a prairie fire can burn a dugout. Most likely your wife and boy're safe enough, if they had sense enough to stay indoors."

Apparently such a thought had never crossed the sodbuster's mind. It didn't seem possible that any living thing could have survived the holocaust, and Dutch admitted to himself that the chances were pretty slim.

The farmer rubbed his face with a shaking hand. "Mister, I got to go now. Back to the east there's a new section line road; you'll be able to catch somebody there that'll give you a ride." He whipped up his bony team and the wagon jolted recklessly toward the huge stretches of burned-out grass.

As much as he needed and wanted a ride, Dutch let him go without a word. There was something about the sodbuster's long face and sorrowful eyes that had taken the edge off of Dutch's good humor. "Just let him go," he said aloud, leaning on his crutch. "I don't need no long-faced sodbuster to ruin the day for me." He began hobbling off to the east.

As he looked for the road he tried to bring back that rosy glow of good cheer that he had felt when the fire overtook the medicine man's wagon. But it would not return. He fell into a fit of moody, unfocused anger. His leg began to swell, and the pain was like knives through his knee. The dead sorrel, his injured knee, his lost job—they were all the fault of the medicine man. The longer Dutch dwelled on this thought the harder it was to bear and the angrier he became, because the medicine man was dead. And there was no way of avenging a hurt, no matter how grave, on a dead man.

By the time he reached the road—which was no more than a meandering wagon track—Dutch Rainey was in a black, savage mood. It was a poor time for a young and inexperienced sheriff's deputy like Whit Murphy to cross his path.

Deputy Murphy, a lanky, sandy-haired farmboy, would have been twenty-one later that month—if he had lived. He was wearing his badge as a temporary thing, just until his pa got the crops in that fall. To tell the truth, Whit was not much of a lawman. He was an easygoing young man whose nature leaned more toward plows than guns. Still, the wages of a deputy in a newly organized Territory was better than nothing, which was what he had been making on the farm. And, of course, there was always the chance of collecting a reward, if you were a lawman. As it turned out, it was the business of rewards that brought Deputy Murphy to his ruin.

Earlier that day a Kansas cowman and two of his hands had come to Whit with a complaint of horse theft. Whit, if he had lived to be a hundred, never would have understood the working of a cowman's mind. This rancher had left his outfit in Kansas and brought two of his men all the way down to the Territory because of the loss of a single horse. On top of that he was offering a reward of one hundred dollars for the capture of the horse thief. To Whit's mind the loss of a single saddle animal simply was not worth all that bother and expense. But Whit was not a cowman.

There was not even anything special about the animal. "Sorrel," the rancher—a grim faced man by the name of Matthew Silver—had told him. "White forestockings, about six years old. My Quarter Circle-S brand is on the right hip."

"Well," Whit had said doubtfully, "I'll keep my eyes open. If I see the animal I'll put it up for you."

"I'm not interested in the sorrel," the cowman said in his harsh, angry way. "It's the man I want, and it's the man I'll pay for."

This was a shocking statement to Deputy Murphy who valued livestock above gold and silver, second only to land. But Whit had learned that it did no good to get upset when dealing with cowmen. "All right, Mr. Silver," he said mildly, "I'll keep my eyes open for the man too. What does he look like?"

Matthew Silver's description of the thief had been much more precise than his description of the horse. "Tolerably tall, about six feet. Pinkish hair, what little there is of it. Pale, whey colored eyes. He'll have a rifle on his saddle and a .45 on his hip. But the way you'll know him is the blue bandanna he'll have on his head."

Whit had accepted without comment, as if it were the most common thing in the world to run across pink-haired men wearing blue bandannas on their heads. "All right," he said, smiling pleasantly, "I'll look out for him."

"You better look out for his gun too, if you find him. His name's Dutch Rainey, and he ain't one of your psalm-shoutin' sodbusters. He's mad and he's mean."

"I'll remember," the young deputy told him absently. As a matter of fact he didn't give himself a fiddler's chance of collecting that bounty. It was a big prairie between Wichita and Oklahoma Territory; it didn't seem likely that he and the bandanna-wearing horse thief would be crossing paths.

Which only went to prove how wrong a man's figuring can be.

Deputy Murphy had been looking into a case of fence cutting and was now returning to his headquarters in Plateau when he first saw the stranger by the side of the road. A stranger tolerably tall, about six feet. With pink-colored hair, what Whit could see of it beneath the blue bandanna that the man wore on his head. Young Whit Murphy could not have been more surprised if a bright green fox or a scarlet cougar had suddenly crossed his path.

But he recovered quickly, with visions of hundred dollars rewards in his head. As he closed the distance between them to something less than twenty yards, Whit grabbed his saddle rifle out of the boot and said loudly, "Put your hands in the air, mister!"

It was the first time he had ever thrown down on a man, and the words sounded slightly ridiculous and pompous. The stranger, much to the deputy's consternation, merely lifted his chin and looked at him with a pair of the palest eyes that he had ever seen.

"I said put your hands up!" Whit repeated, this time in a shout.

The stranger continued to look at him but didn't raise his hands. His pale eyes seemed to focus on the deputy's badge, a slightly tarnished nickel-plated shield which was pinned like a target over Whit Murphy's heart.

"You made a mistake," the stranger said at last. "You got me mixed up with somebody else."

"I ain't makin' no mistake! Your name's Dutch Rainey, and you're wanted for stealin' a sorrel horse from your boss' place up by Wichita! Put up your hands or I'll shoot!"

Dutch's face remained blank, but he grinned to himself. Very slowly, he raised his hands. "Whatever you say, Deputy. I don't aim to cause no trouble. Maybe you wouldn't mind tellin' me somethin'."

Murphy scowled. His nervous roan sidestepped and it took the young lawman several seconds to settle the animal down. While this was happening, his rifle was pointing at various indefinite points on the open prairie. Dutch watched it all with tolerant amusement; there was no doubt in his mind he could kill that young plowboy deputy any time he took the notion.

"Now," Whit Murphy sternly told his prisoner, as soon as he got his saddle animal settled down, "I want you to drop your gun."

"How," Dutch smiled, "do you aim for me to do that, with my hands up in the air?"

"Well, you can let them down long enough to unbuckle your belt. But be careful, I'm watchin' you."

Dutch pretended not to understand what he was talking about. "Who was it that told you about me, Deputy? You got the drop on me, it won't hurt anything to tell."

"It was your boss, a cowman by the name of Silver, and two of his hands. Now let go of your .45."

Dutch was only mildly surprised that Matthew Silver would ride all the way from Wichita looking for a single horse. Cattlemen could be mighty touchy on the subject of stolen livestock—the bigger the cattleman the touchier he was apt to be. Still, there was nothing to be disturbed about. It was a big prairie. Tomorrow, with a fresh horse under him, he would make for Indian Territory and maybe on to Arkansas. That would be the end of it.

"I don't aim to tell you again," the young lawman said nervously. "Unbuckle your gunbelt, mister."

Dutch looked up at him and grinned widely. The roan, already skitterish, could feel that he had a nervous and frightened rider on his back. Dutch began walking forward, lowering his arms slowly. The roan began to shy.

It was all so easy that Dutch hardly gave it a thought. As the deputy—plowboy that he was—began sawing on the reins, Dutch simply drew his .45 and shot him.

Shot him and forgot about him.

Dutch limped forward quickly, grabbed the roan's head stall and hauled the animal down with no nonsense. Young Whit Murphy, his face a startled mask, was just beginning to dump out of the saddle. He fell to the ground and the roan dragged him in a tight half circle until Dutch punched his foot out of the stirrup. "Mister," Dutch told him indifferently, "you made your big mistake the day you left the farm." He picked up the rifle, a Marlin 30-30 in reasonably good condition.

Whit Murphy looked up with dead, wide-open eyes, as Dutch climbed painfully into the saddle and, without a backward look, rode away.

California Sam and his two companions made a hungry camp that night on what appeared to be another fresh-water branch of the Little Arkansas. "If we had a gun we could have us a turkey supper," Hassle said, listening to the big birds settling down to roost in the cottonwoods.

"Well, we ain't got a gun," the medicine man told him. "Scout around and see what you can find."

While Hassle scouted the creekbank the pitchman made a fire. He thought longingly of the sack of Arbuckle coffee that had gone up with the wagon.

"Will we make the railroad town tomorrow?" Rose McGee asked.

"Sometime tomorrow mornin', if my figgerin's right."

"Then what are you goin' to do?"

Sam scratched the cactus-like stubble on his jaw and thought for a while. "I guess I'll wait and see what kind of town it is. A high pitchman always thinks of somethin'."

"A high pitchman with no money, or wagon, or team, or supplies?"

The medicine man shrugged. "Wagons and teams are just flash. A good pitchman don't need them. In San Francisco I pitched from the back of a rented hack and the suckers might nigh trampled each other forcin' their money on me."

"Even if you had the money to rent a hack, how would you get supplies? What kind of merchandise would you sell?"

"Ma'am," Sam told her in his roundest tones, "a real pitchman can sell fresh air and blue sky, and I ain't anything at all if I ain't a first-class pitchman." He looked at her for a minute. Her face was haggard, her eyes red and tired, which was not very surprising, considering the kind of day they had had. He turned his gaze to the fire. "What do you aim to do," he asked, "when we get to Pond Creek?"

She shrugged. "Where there's saloons there's jobs for saloon girls."

"I guess," Sam agreed. They fell into an exhausted silence. After having survived a prairie fire, nothing else seemed worth talking about.

Hassle returned from his scout of the creekbank with a hatful of green persimmons, half ripe plums, and some possum grapes as hard as buckshot. Glumly, they ate a few of the puckery plums and went to sleep.

The next morning they awoke wet with dew and chilled to the bone. They were listless and slack-faced, unrefreshed by the hours of deathlike sleep. Hassle, again exploring the creek bottom, returned with ripe red berries. But not even food succeeded in brightening their outlook or easing their many aches and pains.

"Well," California Sam said at last, "that railroad ain't goin' to come to us, we got to go to it." He hauled himself off the ground and, without another word, tramped off across the prairie.

It was almost noon when Hassle and Rose McGee caught up with him. They were gasping for breath and sweating freely, but at least the color of life was back in their faces.

"I thought you said we'd raise Pond Creek this mornin'!" Hassle said indignantly.

"I'm a pitchman, boy," California Sam told him aloofly, "not a fortuneteller. But sooner or later, if we keep goin' west, we'll come to the railroad. And the railroad'll take us to Pond Creek."

They came to the railroad shortly after midday. Far to the south they could just make out the maze of cattle shipping pens, and the pitchman heaved a huge sigh of relief. "There she is, fellers, and a purtier sight I almost never saw!

Look at her sharp, you can almost see the yokels beggin' to get theirselves fleeced."

To young Hassle Jones, Pond Creek was a bitter disappointment. He had expected a big city, the shuffling of great locomotives, the mill of city traffic. What he saw beyond the shipping pens was a few unpainted shacks of rawhide lumber, a water tower, and a mustard-colored depot. Compared to Wichita, it was no town at all.

To Rose McGee it was just another rawhide town broiling under a July sun. One place was much the same as any other when all you saw of it was the inside of the nearest saloon.

Only California Sam was cheered to any considerable degree in what he saw of Pond Creek, Oklahoma Territory. His long face brightened, his watery eyes cleared amazingly, the spring of youth was in his shambling gait. "Stirs the old juices, don't it?" he said happily. "Nothin' like a nest of suckers to liven the spirit and put a tingle in the blood."

"I don't see any suckers," Hassle complained moodily.

"You will, boy. You will. One thing California Sam can do is smell out a flock of yokels, like an old hound dog treein' a coon."

"I don't see what good it's goin' to do. How are you goin' to pitch when you ain't got nothin' to sell?"

"Boy," the pitchman scolded him mildly, "you got to have faith. You got to be ready to step right in and grab opportunity by the horns. Because there's always an opportunity hidin' back in the corner somewheres, you just got to know how to recognize it when you see it."

They approached the town from the north, walking the green, pitch-oozing crossties. "Hell and damnation!" the pitchman muttered as he stumbled and almost fell. The roadbed was new and unsettled, like everything else in the Territory. The gleaming steel rails couldn't seem to make up their minds whether they wanted to stay together or each go its own way.

Hassle complained bitterly, but mostly to himself. His shoes in poor condition to begin with, had all but burned off his feet in the prairie fire. The hot rosin oozing from the green ties blistered his soles, but the sharp gravel alongside the rails were even worse. Rose McGee—whose red-top shoes were in even worse shape than Hassle's—took the boy's hand and said, "Hold on a spell longer. We'll get new shoes in Pond Creek."

"How can we buy anything?" the boy demanded. "There ain't none of us got any money."

"There's ways," the saloon woman told him with a crooked smile. "There's ways."

California Sam, for the most part, ignored the grumbling of his companions. His pitchman's nose twitched expectantly. A hundred subtle schemes and treacheries whirled in his mind. Somehow there was a way—there was always a way—to separate a yokel from his money, and there was no doubt in his mind that California Sam was just the pitchman to find it.

He began to hum a cheerful little tune, striding several paces ahead of Hassle and Rose. But as they drew closer to the town, the humming stopped. A deep scowl settled on his long bristling face. Something was wrong. What it was he couldn't say exactly, but a medicine man learned to sense these things about a town.

He pulled up short and stood there for several seconds, his head cocked on one shoulder, his watery eyes vague and unfocused. He sniffed the air like an old prairie lobo sniffing out a motherless calf. Hassle and Rose, in their half blind, plodding way, almost ran over him.

"What's the matter?" Rose asked in vague alarm. For a moment she thought the pitchman had been taken with a fit of some kind.

"I ain't sure," Sam told her, "but somethin's stirrin'. I can feel it in the air." He nudged Hassle. "You got good eyes, boy. Tell me what you see up ahead."

Hassle studied the town for some time. "Well," he said at last, "there ain't much doin' on the streets that I can see. There's a train at the depot, and what looks like a lot of steam. The steam's comin' from the train engine, I guess."

"Dammit, boy," Sam said impatiently, "I can see the train. I ain't *that blind*. What else do you see?"

"Some people at the depot. I can't tell how many."

The pitchman squinted hard and tried to see for himself, but the details of the scene were blurred and indistinct. "How many people would you say, boy?"

Hassle shrugged. "Hard to tell. Most of them are hid behind that cloud of steam."

Slowly, the pitchman's face began to brighten. "Trouble!" he said happily. "There's been trouble! Hurry up, we got no time to lose!"

As they approached the outskirts of town the scene began to take shape. There had been a minor collision of a freight locomotive and a switch engine. A boiler had ruptured, which accounted for the clouds of steam and the curious spectators. With the confidence of a man long experienced in grabbing opportunity by the horns, the pitchman urged his companions on. "Hurry up, we got to get there before the commotion settles."

"Why are we in such a hurry to look at a train wreck?" Rose asked wearily.

"Don't ask fool questions! There ain't no time for that now!"

They straggled into Pond Creek, Sam leading the way. He grabbed the first native he could find and demanded, "Has anybody been hurt?"

The townsman waved his arms excitedly. "Hard to tell in all this steam, but I don't think so!"

"But you ain't sure?"

"Well, no, I ain't sure. Doc Pettiford and the depot agent was lookin' the ground over, but I don't think they found anybody."

"But you never can tell, in an accident like this one," the pitchman said cheerfully. As the native drifted away in the swirling steam, Sam grasped Hassle's hand and pulled him forward. "Foller me, boy! We got to act fast!"

"Hey!" Hassle complained. "You're pullin' my arm out of the socket!"

With a grunt of impatience, Sam let go of his hand. Hassle immediately stumbled over a steel rail and fell sprawling in the gravel. "Dammit, boy," the pitchman groaned, "you got to watch where you're goin'! Are you hurt?"

Hassle sat up and inspected himself for cuts and bruises. "Just this place on my head," he said at last, fingering a small cut over his right eye. To his amazement, California Sam clapped him on the back and grinned widely. "Boy, I couldn't made a better pitch if I'd sat up all night writin' it! Now lay down. Lay still and don't say a word till I tell you."

Hassle blinked in surprise. "What're you talkin' about?"

With a huge sigh of impatience, the pitchman hollered, "Dammit, boy, when are you goin' to learn not to ask questions? Just lay down and do like I tell you!"

The boy still was not satisfied with the way things were going, but he lay back on the white gravel beside the tracks. Through the steam he could see the two locomotives locked together like bull buffaloes in a fight to the death. Probably an inexperienced switchman, he guessed, for he had seen such accidents before in Wichita.

"Now listen to me, son," the pitchman said, squinting at the shadowy figures of natives through curtains of moist steam. They all seemed to be running from place to place and hollering excitedly. "Now listen to me," Sam said again in a quiet, calm voice. "I'm goin' to get you a doc. You got hurt when them two locomotives run together. Maybe a piece of iron flew off of one of the engines and hit you—hard to say, with all this commotion. You just lay there and be quiet and don't say a word, you understand?"

"You aim to beat the railroad out of some money," Hassle said promptly. He was beginning to understand the pitchman better than Sam realized.

"Boy," California Sam told him sternly, "I worry about you. You got a suspicious mind. Now you lay there and don't move, because I'm goin' to start doin' some hollerin'." With that pithy lecture delivered, the pitchman rose to his feet and began bellowing, "I want a doctor! This boy's been hurt! I want a doctor!"

There was a great deal of milling on the part of the natives, but the pitchman kept hollering at the top of his lungs, "I want a doctor! This boy's hurt!"

After several minutes of uproar a large, beefy man in a shapeless black suit, stepped up and said, "I'm a doctor. You can stop that infernal bellowin'."

Sam obliged by stopping the hollering. It had served its purpose, having attracted a good-sized crowd of yokels to the scene of the "accident."

The doctor knelt beside Hassle and inspected him for several minutes. "There's nothin' wrong with this boy, except for a scratch on his forehead."

"He's hurt, I tell you!" Sam started again. "He's bleedin'! He can't move. What kind of doctor are you?"

The natives crowded in to have a closer look. Sure enough, there was a small amount of blood on the youth's forehead. They nodded their heads knowingly.

A second man stepped out of the crowd, waded through the clouds of steam and touched the pitchman on the shoulder. "Here, you've made enough racket. The doctor's lookin' after the boy. Are you the father?"

This was a ticklish point, but Sam was prepared for it. "Not his father, exactly. The poor lad don't have a family of his own. I'm his guardine."

"You got papers to prove that?"

"Of course," the pitchman intoned loftily, "I got the papers. Unfortunately, we got caught in a prairie fire and lost my wagon. The papers was in the wagon."

"I guess you can get more papers if you have to."

"Of course I can get more papers!" The pitchman eyed the man indignantly. He was a gaunt, sour-faced bird with a puckered mouth and eyes like small round stones. The depot agent. The best part of his life had been spent watching people come and go on trains, all kinds of people. His expression indicated that he had not found many good ones among them.

The agent knelt down beside the doctor who was now listening to Hassle's thin chest with a stethoscope. "What about it, Doc, is he all right?"

The doctor stuffed the stethoscope in his satchel. "His breathin's a little irregular, heart's a little fast. Most likely it's just the excitement—still, it wouldn't hurt to take him somewhere and keep an eye on him for a spell."

An alarmed Rose McGee had at last found her way through the curtains of steam and was clawing at the pitchman's sleeve. "What happened here? What's wrong with Hassle?"

"Nothin'," Sam assured her. Then, for the benefit of the yokels, he quickly added, "Nothin' *serious*, that is. At least, we *hope* not."

Rose stared at Hassle who lay rigidly beside the track, his eyes tightly shut. "What do you mean, we *hope* he ain't hurt?"

The medicine man growled to himself. Comforting excitable women was a luxury that the present situation did not allow. "I mean we hope he ain't hurt *bad*," Sam explained for the benefit of the doctor and the depot agent and a good number of natives who were now watching the two of them. "As any fool can plainly see, the boy's *hurt*." Then, before the saloon woman got a chance to ask more awkward questions, the pitchman started hollering again,

"I want an ambulance! We got to get this boy to a hospital! I want an ambulance!"

The doctor hauled himself to his feet. "The closest ambulance," he told the pitchman, "is in Oklahoma City. The closest hospital too. But I've got a sick room over the feed store; we can take the boy there."

The depot agent's gaunt face was flushed with outrage. "This is a flim-flam, Doc! A scheme to sucker the railroad out of some money."

"Look at the blood on the lad's head!" Sam hollered indignantly. "*That* ain't flim-flam!"

"There'll be hell to pay," the agent warned, "if we let them get away with this."

California Sam pulled himself up to his full height, an impressive picture of righteousness outraged. "Are you goin' to let the poor boy lay there bleedin', maybe dyin', because the big, rich railroad don't want to help him?"

The doctor smiled apologetically at the agent. "Sorry, Lloyd, but I can't just let him lay there." He nodded to the pitchman. "Give me a hand. We'll carry him across the street to my place."

They picked Hassle up between them and carried him across the dusty street and up a flight of outside stairs to the doctor's sick room. The two men carefully lay the boy on a small iron cot, and the doctor, whose name was Pettiford, said, "You and the woman wait outside. I'll let you know when I'm through lookin' the boy over."

Obediently, the pitchman took Rose by the arm and led her out to the landing at the top of the stairs. Rose was so tense that her eyes bulged. "Damn you!" she hissed under her breath. "If you don't tell me what you're tryin' to pull I'm goin' to start screamin'!"

"Gentle down," Sam told her nervously. "Everything's fine. The boy ain't hurt."

"Then why was you makin' all that racket?"

"Because," the pitchman told her with infinite patience,

"any time you see an accident that involves a railroad or a stage company or a big express outfit, the best thing to do is lay down and start hollerin'. Most likely there's money in it."

Rose stared at him in amazement. "You schemed all this from the beginnin'!"

The pitchman heaved one of his ponderous sighs. Reasoning with women was a difficult undertaking under the best of conditions; when they were excited it was all but impossible. However, he forced himself to make the effort. "Maybe it's slipped your mind," he said, with just a hint of sarcasm, "that we was caught in a prairie fire not long back. Everything was lost—wagon, team, money. Even the clothes on our backs is burned full of holes. Of course . . ." He paused, and his tone became acid. "Of course, if I had that diamond stickpin that I used to have, there wouldn't be no trouble. Unfortunately I don't have that stickpin any more."

It was Rose's turn to sigh. She had long since given up the hope that he would ever let her forget about that stickpin. "I don't like the idea of usin' Hassle this way. I'll find a saloon and make enough money to get us out of here."

California Sam regarded her thoughtfully. Under ordinary conditions Rose McGee was not a hard-looking woman, but at the moment she was the worse for wear. Soot and grime were ground into her face; her hair was singed and flying wildly, like a swarm of gnats, about her head. And her recent experience with Alf Ritter had done nothing to improve her looks, either—it had left her eyes dull, her spirit slack.

The pitchman said with unexpected gentleness, "This time let me do things my way."

"You always have to do things *your* way, don't you?" She was quietly bitter but not slashing.

"This time it's better. Do you know what that depot agent is doin' right now? He's over at the depot gettin' an urgent message off to the office in Oklahoma City. Sometime tomorrow a railroad lawyer will get off the train and look us up. He won't be in a happy frame of mind; most likely he'll do considerable hollerin' and threatenin' before he finally comes around. But he'll come around . . . If he's not pressed too hard."

"How do you know that?"

"Because it's a lot cheaper than goin' to court. Because goin' to court would be bad publicity for the railroad. Because yokels are quick to believe the worst about railroads." He put on a long face and looked down at the natives who were watching them curiously. "Humor me, and don't ask any more fool questions. I know what I'm doin'."

"What about Hassle?"

"Hassle's stretched out in a clean bed, where I'd like to be right now. I wouldn't worry too much about the boy. He's tough."

"He wasn't so tough when he got those scars on his back."

On that thought they fell into a gloomy silence.

7

THE doctor came out of the sick room and fixed Sam and Rose with a suspicious eye. "I still can't find anything wrong with the boy, but he can stay in bed tonight and I'll look at him again tomorrow."

"Thank you, Doc." California Sam lunged up from the top step where he had been sitting. "Is it all right if we talk to him now?"

"It's all right with me," Doc Pettiford said sourly. "I couldn't get anything out of him but grunts."

"You done fine!" the pitchman told Hassle as soon as he entered the room. "The doc don't know what to think; that's a good sign. I couldn't of done better myself."

"I'm hungry," Hassle said.

"I'll get you the best meal Pond Creek can afford," the pitchman told him. "You lay right there and don't talk to anybody."

"Can't I talk to Rose?"

"To Rose but nobody else. What do you feel like in the way of grub?"

"Steak," the youth told him without hesitation. "Fried steak and cream potatoes and gravy, and some peach cobbler on the side."

The pitchman laughed approvingly. "I couldn't of done a better job of orderin' myself. I'll be back before you know it."

Hassle looked at Rose as the medicine man went out the door. "How's he goin' to buy grub without any money?"

"I don't know," Rose said with her crooked smile. "But I expect he'll manage." She moved to the cot and touched the boy's head lightly. "You're all right, ain't you? You ain't got a fever or anything like that?"

"I'm fine," Hassle told her. "Just hungry."

It occurred to Rose that she was hungry too. She could hardly remember the time she had tasted food more substantial than wild berries. She took a chair beside the cot and kicked off her charred shoes. "Lord," she sighed, "I feel older'n the hills. It seems like a year since I started on the road with that crazy pitchman!"

"Maybe time enough to forget about Alf Ritter?" Hassle asked.

For a moment she looked blank. Then she sagged back in the chair and shook her head in amazement. "I had to stop a minute and think who Alf Ritter was. How long's it been since he was supposed to come for me—three, four days? Might as well be a lifetime. The kind of time you count on a calendar don't mean much when you travel with a man like California Sam." She shook her head again. "A few days ago I was ready to kill myself because of Alf. Now I don't care if I ever see him again. I just don't care."

Hassle looked at her thoughtfully. "You kind of like the pitchman, don't you?"

The thought seemed to startle her. "Like him? Well, most

men would of had me arrested for stealin' that diamond stickpin—I guess I like him for not doin' that."

"I like him," Hassle said in the same thoughtful tone. "The first time I seen him he beat me out of a dollar. Then, before I knew what he was up to, he got me to help him beat a hotel out of their rent money. I thought I hated him." He shrugged. "But I didn't. He's smart. That's one reason I like him."

"Like an old he-coyote he's smart. He'd steal the pennies off a dead man's eyes."

"Maybe," the boy agreed. "But what does a dead man need with pennies?"

When the pitchman returned to the sick room, Hassle and Rose McGee were chattering with great animation. "Well," the medicine man said cheerfully, "this here's a right lively soundin' place for a sick room."

"What you got there?" Hassle asked, looking at a large cloth-covered plate that Sam had in his hands.

"Just what you ordered, boy. Fried steak, cream potatoes, gravy, and bakin' powder biscuits. There's even some peach cobbler." He whipped off the cloth like a head waiter at the Windsor in Denver.

Stunned and delighted, Hassle stared at the mountain of food. But Rose McGee, suspicious as ever, demanded, "How did you do it, without any money?"

"Easiest thing in the world," the pitchman beamed at them. "Down the street there's a grand lady by the name of Mrs. Lawson. Runs a boardin'house. A kinder-hearted lady there never was—I thought she was goin' to bust out in tears when I told her about the poor boy that got run over by a train and was half starvin' and didn't have any money because of gettin' caught in a prairie fire." California Sam favored them with a face-splitting grin. "Oh, she was sorry for the poor boy, all right, but she didn't start cookin' that grub till I told her about the railroad lawyer comin' tomorrow to settle with us for the accident. Remember that, son.

Railroads, along with banks and express companies, are as good as money in the pocket, if folks think you're takin' them to court."

Hassle stared at him with admiration. "I'll remember."

"Good. Here, dig in."

Sam put the heavy plate on Hassle's lap and grinned happily as the boy eagerly cut off a piece of steak and stuffed it in his mouth. Without bothering to chew, he loaded a fork with potatoes and gravy, shoved it into his mouth and immediately followed it with a bite of biscuit.

"That's enough," Sam said, whisking the plate away.

Hassle almost choked. "What're you doin'? I ain't even *started* to eat yet!"

"You're sick, boy," the pitchman told him in fatherly tones. "What would that railroad lawyer think tomorrow if he found out you cleaned up a big plate of grub the first hour you was in the sick room. You know what he'd do? He'd go right over to the depot and send a telegram to Oklahoma City. 'The boy ain't sick.' That's what he'd tell them. 'Don't pay them a penny.' Well, we can't let that happen, can we?"

Hassle groaned. "I ain't goin' to get nothin' to eat for the rest of the day?"

"Don't you fret about a thing, boy. Old Sam ain't goin' to let you starve. Here." He shoved a four inch amber stick under the youth's nose.

"What's that?" Hassle demanded suspiciously.

"Hoarhound candy, son, what does it look like? A soft-hearted yokel in the general store gave it to me to give to the boy that was hit by the train. Eat 'er down!"

The boy eyed the candy as if it were poison. "Is this all I'm going to get?"

"Nothin' like candy to settle a growlin' stomach." Sam recovered the still full plate with the luncheon cloth. "I'll just take this back to that kind-hearted lady, Mrs. Lawson, and tell her thanks just the same, but the poor boy's too sick to eat. Inside an hour it'll be all over town. Everybody knows that a boy that don't eat is sure enough sick. Let the lawyer knock his head against *that* tomorrow."

Rose grinned her crooked grin at Hassle as California Sam went out the door. "There goes your smart pitchman. What do you think about him now?"

Hassle bit off a piece of the hard candy and chewed without enthusiasm. "I guess I like him all right. But sometimes it ain't easy!"

The pitchman, his long face at its longest, quietly let it be known around town that the boy's condition was grave—and he could point to the still full plate of food to prove it.

When he returned to the sick room he delivered a brief lecture to Rose and Hassle. "There's one thing you always got to remember when dealin' with natives. As long as a sucker believes he's goin' to get somethin' for nothin' you'll have him eatin' out of your hand. The yokels out there . . ." He indicated, with a generous gesture, the entire world outside the sick room. "The yokels out there are convinced we'll get rich off the railroad, then they'll get rich outfittin' us with all the things we need. As long as they think that, the town's ours."

"Are we goin' to get rich off the railroad?" Rose asked.

"No," the pitchman told her without hesitation. "We may get a free ticket out of town, and a few dollars to pay the doc and the other bills that we run up, but that's all. Railroads never got to be the biggest business in the country by givin' their money away."

To young Hassle Jones, this was a bitter revelation. "If that's all we can expect, it don't hardly seem worth the bother."

"A free railroad ticket and a few dollars is better'n nothin', boy," the pitchman told him heartily. "By a *considerable* sight!"

Because Sam had decided that it wouldn't be seemly for concerned parents (or even guardians) to be seen eating while their boy teetered at death's door, they joined Hassle in fasts of their own. By morning all three of them were feeling slightly dizzy.

Rose and the pitchman had spent a restless night in the sick room, Sam in the chair, Rose on a makeshift pallet on the floor. The medicine man awoke to the rumbling of his own stomach. "Godamighty!" he groaned. "When was the last time I et? I can't even remember!"

"The berries," Hassle reminded him.

"The berries," California Sam repeated. That seemed like half a lifetime ago. "Well," he sighed, "I'll go get you some breakfast."

"What good will it do, if I can't eat it?"

"Appearances, boy. Got to keep up appearances."

Mrs. Lawson prepared a stack of six flapjacks, two fried eggs, two thick slabs of smoked bacon, a large pitcher of sorghum molasses, and a pot of black coffee. "The coffee's for you and the missus," the thoughtful boardinghouse keeper told the pitchman. "I know you won't feel like eatin', bein' worried as you must be about the boy."

"Thank you, ma'am," Sam told her weakly. "That's real kind of you."

"You and the missus expectin' the railroad lawyer anytime soon?"

"Sometime today, I expect, Mrs. Lawson."

Mrs. Lawson favored him with a motherly smile. "Good. I expect you and the missus will be feelin' better after talkin' to the lawyer. Why don't you let me fix you a good meal as soon as you get your appetite back?"

"Thank you, ma'am, we'll do that."

"Cagy old biddy, our Mrs. Lawson," the pitchman reported to his companions when he returned to the sick room. "Same as threatened to starve us to death if the lawyer don't bring us some money today."

In an atmosphere heavy with gloom, Hassle took a single bite from one flapjack, nicked one egg with a fork and handed the plate back to Sam. The three of them sat drinking black coffee, too concerned with their rumbling stomachs to make conversation.

At last Rose turned a disapproving glance on Hassle and said, "I ain't sure an eleven-year-old boy ought to be drinkin' coffee."

"If it helps settle the growlin' in his stomach, he is," Hassle told her.

Around midmorning Doc Pettiford returned to his sick room to check on the patient. "Well," he said dryly, "the boy seems to be holdin' his own. He'd feel better if he had some breakfast."

"He tried but couldn't get much down, Doc," Sam told him sorrowfully.

Pettiford looked at the three of them from beneath his shaggy brows. He didn't say what he was thinking.

Early that afternoon the Rock Island northbound huffed to a stop in front of the depot. It was a big day for Pond Creek—the natives had come out early to see the service engine haul away the damaged locomotive while an emergency crew repaired the faulty switch. Most of them were staying to see if the lawyer arrived on the northbound.

Sam was not encouraged when the gangly, stringbean of a man stepped down from the iron steps of the day coach and went directly to the Pond Creek operator. They talked for several minutes while the natives looked on expectantly. At last Lloyd Toom, the local ticket agent and telegraph operator, guided the stranger through the crowd, making directly for the pitchman.

"This here's the man I was tellin' you about," the operator said to the lawyer. "Calls hisself California Sam. Him and the woman called Rose McGee, and the boy by the name of

Hassle Jones, landed here yesterday right after the accident."

"Right *before* the accident," Sam corrected him mildly.

The operator smiled acidly. "Anyway, this is the man, Mr. Lackley."

The lawyer turned to the pitchman and sized him up with a steely eye. "Adam Lackley, sir," he said, looking as if he were slowly strangling in his high stiff collar. "I represent the railroad."

"How do you do, Mr. Lackley," Sam told him politely. I'm California Sam and I represent the boy, Hassle Jones."

"You're not the boy's father, as I understand it."

"That's right. I'm the boy's guardine, like I explained to the operator yesterday."

"But you have no papers to prove that."

"The papers went up with my wagon in a prairie fire."

The lawyer shrugged. "The woman that's with you, Rose McGee. Is she the boy's mother?"

"No, she's just a woman that got stranded on the prairie, and me and the boy was givin' her a ride when we struck the fire."

Mr. Adam Lackley pulled a long face to show what he thought of *that* story. "Well, at any rate . . ." He paused and tapped a front tooth with the tip of his finger. "At any rate, the fact that the boy was not on the scene at the time of the accident yesterday is easily established. Although the railroad admits no fault, we are willing to settle with the doctor for examining the boy, and pay for the rent of the sick room. Please sign here."

Like a magician producing a fluttering dove out of thin air, the lawyer produced an official-looking document and an indelible pencil. The pitchman grinned. "That's lettin' the railroad off pretty light, ain't it?"

"The railroad owes you absolutely nothing, Mr. . . . Mr. Sam."

"You might be right," Sam admitted. "On the other hand,

maybe not. I think I'll telegraph my lawyer in Oklahoma City before I sign any papers."

The lawyer's face became a stone mask. "You're making a mistake, sir. A very grave mistake. Attempt to defraud is a serious matter in this Territory."

The pitchman smiled noncommittally. "I was hopin' the railroad would be a little more generous."

"Not a penny, sir," the lawyer told him grimly.

California Sam heaved a ponderous sigh. "There's nothin' for it, then, I'll have to telegraph my lawyer. Operator, if you'll just step into the depot I'll write it out for you."

Adam Lackley did not blink an eye, but his face became a trifle pale. "You are pursuing a dangerous course, sir. I warn you, the Rock Island Railroad is not a company to be dallied with."

"I think we better get that telegram on the wire," the medicine man smiled to the operator. He strolled to the depot, with the deeply scowling operator and lawyer following a step behind. The natives watched with bugging eyes. It looked like the pitchman was winning out over the railroad, and this was something that didn't happen every day.

Inside the depot Sam got a telegraph form and began to write. Through clinched teeth, Adam Lackley said, "Many men have tried to make themselves rich at the railroad's expense, with tragic results, sir. Tragic results."

The pitchman continued to write. "I never said I wanted to get rich."

Lackley cocked his head to one side, like a hawk, his mind racing. If that telegram went out, if a lawyer did come, if a case was actually made against the railroad and it came to court, there would be hell to pay with the lawyer's employers. In a slightly milder voice, he asked, "Just what have you got in mind, sir?"

"A fair deal, that's all." The pitchman signed the telegraph form.

"What do you consider a fair deal?"

"Well . . ." Sam looked up and appeared to think about it for the first time. "Like I said before, I lost my wagon in the fire. Do you think the railroad could let go of three tickets to Oklahoma City?"

The lawyer's eyes were dark with suspicion. "Is that all?"

"Just about. There's a little bill with the boardin'house, and with Doc Pettiford."

Grudgingly, the lawyer nodded. "The company will take care of them for you."

"We'll need some new clothes."

"You won't get them with railroad money," Lackley told him coldly.

"And some travelin' money," the pitchman continued, as though he had suddenly gone deaf. "Say about a hundred dollars."

"Absolutely not."

Sam smiled sadly at the operator. "Send the telegram."

"Wait a minute." The lawyer spat, as if he had bitten into a wormy apple. There was no doubt in his mind that he could beat the case in court—but it would be an expensive satisfaction. "Twenty dollars," he managed, with considerable difficulty.

"Sixty," the pitchman echoed.

"Thirty," Lackley grated. "And that's my last word." Sam quietly studied the lawyer's face, the throbbing blue veins in his temples, the bulging eyes. He decided that Adam Lackley had been pushed to the edge. Best to stop and take what he could.

Hassle and Rose McGee were sitting in glum silence when the pitchman burst into the sick room. "There you are!" the medicine man beamed, dumping an armload of parcels onto the bed. "California Sam promised you grub, and California Sam's a man of his word! Dig in, eat all you can hold. The case is settled."

Young Hassle Jones, ever the practical one, asked, "How much did you get?"

"Three train tickets to Oklahoma City and thirty dollars cash money."

"Thirty dollars!" The boy looked as if he had been slapped. Visions of thousands of dollars had been in his mind.

"Boy," Sam told him with dignity, "it ain't the amount of money that counts, it's how bad you need it. Besides, I was lucky to get anything at all." He sorted through the packages and handed two to Hassle. "Here's a pair of pants and a shirt for you; we'll get you some shoes in Oklahoma City. And here's a dress for you," he said to Rose, handing her a package. "It's cheap goods but it'll see you through the train ride."

"Rose ain't goin'," Hassle said, opening a can of sardines.

California Sam stood for a moment blinking his watery eyes.

Rose said, "I talked to the doc. He says there's two saloons in town; one of them ought to take me on."

The pitchman shrugged. "Well, maybe. But it ain't much of a town. If I talked to the operator maybe I could get him to change one of these Oklahoma City tickets for a Wichita one."

"No." Rose smiled bleakly. "I don't want to go back to Wichita."

"Because of Alf Ritter?"

"Not because of him. It ain't likely he'll ever show his face in that part of Kansas again." She held up her new dress and looked at it critically. It was of faded gray material, with a high neck and a floor-sweeping skirt. Not exactly the thing for a saloon woman, but it would have to do until she could get something better. "Let me know when you get settled; I aim to pay you for that stickpin."

"If you do," the pitchman told her bluntly, "it'll be the first time anybody ever got anything back from a pennyweighter. Well . . ." He shrugged his heavy shoulders. "Here's your ticket. If you change your mind, you can try to get the operator to change it for you."

Rose accepted the ticket and, to Sam's surprise, suddenly laughed. "Don't get me wrong," she told the medicine man. "I'm sorry about the stickpin, and I appreciate everything you've done for me since the time you picked me up on the prairie. It looks like you're the only one that ever went out of his way to help me—that's kind of funny, ain't it?"

"I don't know about that—but it don't speak very well for the brains of medicine men. That much I got to admit."

She rolled up the dress and put it under her arm. "Well, I'll be goin' now."

"Wait a minute," Hassle said, his mouth full of sardines and cheese and crackers. "Don't you want nothin' to eat?"

Rose smiled. "Thanks anyway, Hassle. I guess I ain't hungry."

"You don't have to go right now, do you?"

"No sense puttin' a thing off."

"Why don't you come to Oklahoma City with me and California Sam?"

Rose shook her head. "No, it's time I started lookin' after myself again. It's somethin' you have to keep workin' at or you lose the trick of it. Goodbye, Hassle. Be a good boy." And her faded blue eyes added silently, *Heaven help you. With nobody to look after you but a high-talkin' medicine show pitchman.*

As Rose reached for the door, Hassle stopped her a second time. "Wait a minute." He turned to the pitchman. "Is there any of that thirty dollars left that you got from the lawyer?"

"Four dollars. Little enough to get us started when we land in Oklahoma City."

"You still owe me a dollar for doin' chores for you in Wichita. I want it."

The pitchman was shocked. "Boy, didn't you hear me? We're goin' to need every penny of that money!"

"I want it," Hassle repeated stubbornly. "You owe it to me. You promised it to me. I want it."

With a look of a man who was peeling off a yard of his own skin, California Sam grudgingly took a single greenback from his meager roll. "All right," he said huffily, "if you don't trust old Sam to look after your money for you, there you are!"

"I want Rose to have it."

Something disturbing happened to Rose's face. Slowly, it began to crumple. Her eyes glistened moistly. Sam put the dollar in her hand and muttered, "Well, it's the boy's money, and he wants you to have it. So here it is."

She crushed it in her fist with the train ticket. Then she turned quickly, opened the door and was gone.

California Sam, his long face even longer and more cynical than usual, sat on the edge of the bed and began opening a can of tomatoes with his pocketknife. "There's one pennyweighter we won't never see again—along with my diamond stickpin."

Hassle bit off a giant bite of cheese and chewed rapidly. "I like her," he said when he finally swallowed. "She was good to me when nobody else in Wichita knew I was alive. She'd even take the time to talk to me."

"Common saloon woman," the pitchman drawled sourly. "Fine kind of company for a boy your age to be keepin'." Expertly, he chopped the tomatoes with the blade of his knife, then turned up the can and drank some of the juice. "You want some?" he asked, offering the can to the boy.

"No. I wish Rose would come with us to Oklahoma City."

"Count your blessin's, boy. All women are trouble, but a woman pennyweighter is pure poison."

"Rose ain't a pennyweighter. Not really. It was because of Alf Ritter that she took your stickpin."

"With a thief it's always because of somethin' or other. Eat your grub, boy. We got us some travelin' to do before long."

Somewhere along the line the pitchman had forgotten that he had planned to send the boy back to Wichita as soon as they reached the railroad. Maybe it was because there was nothing for him to go back to now. Not even Rose.

It was somewhere on the western reaches of Black Bear Creek that County Sheriff Will Mawson located the three possemen from Kansas. Matthew Silver was a heavy, humorless man, bulging with hard fat. One of his two hands was Billy Prince, who had once ridden with Dutch Rainey in the Territory. The second hand was Jed Carp, who had been drafted for posse duty because of his reputation as a dead shot with a rifle.

Mawson was not particularly taken with any of them. Although they were all after the same man—a murderer now—Silver and his two men were a little too cold-blooded for the sheriff's taste. A little too interested in salving the cowman's pride, not interested enough in simple justice.

The three cattlemen were hunkered down around a coffee fire, their rifles within easy reach. Mawson approached them cautiously, thoroughly identifying himself before making any sudden moves. When the necessary formalities were over with, the lawman looked at Silver and said, "Your sorrel has been found. At least we think it's yours. Quarter Circle-S on the right hip." He went on to describe the animal in detail.

Silver stood for a moment, his face like stone. Somehow Mawson got the notion that the cowman did not care much about the sorrel but that he would have cared even less if it had been one of his men that died. "Run to death," Silver said at last. "That's Rainey, all right. He never gave a damn for animals. Well," he added with a note of satisfaction, "he must be close by. He couldn't travel far without a saddle animal of some kind."

"He's got one," the sheriff told him with no noticeable change in tone. "He killed a deputy of mine yesterday and took his 30-30 Marlin and a roan gelding."

The cowman threw back his heavy shoulders and glared at the lawman. "You let him get away?" The lawman had committed the unpardonable sin—he had displeased Matthew Silver.

Mawson became strangely pale. "After a mile or so we lost the roan's tracks, but we followed them long enough to see that Rainey was probably headed for Indian Territory. I started my deputies ahead to warn the Cherokee light horse police . . ." He paused and shrugged defensively. "But there's not much they can do. Once he crosses into Indian country it's a matter for the federal deputies."

"It's a matter for Matthew Silver," the cowman told him coldly. He turned and looked at Billy Prince. "Billy, you and Dutch Rainey was pals once. You must have some notion about where he would go."

Billy scratched his chin nervously. He was well aware that it was poor business to rile Matthew Silver. On the other hand, crossing Dutch Rainey could be fatal.

"Well?" the impatient cowman snapped.

"There's a woman over in the Cherokee Nation," Billy said slowly. "Her and Dutch kind of took to one another when we rode through there a year ago. Might be he's headed to see her again."

The cowman grinned. "There you are, Sheriff. Get your men together; we'll all ride down to the Cherokee Nation and give Dutch a hand with his courtin'."

But at that particular moment Dutch Rainey did not have courting on his mind. For almost an hour he had been quietly watching a mail hack crawl west to east across the prairie. It was a light rig with a fixed top and roll-up canvas curtains. One passenger and the driver.

Dutch's problem was that he was still a long way from the relative safety of the Cherokee Nation. A long way from the comfort of an obliging woman, and—more important—a long way from hot food and a comfortable belly. Deputy Whit Murphy—plowboy that he had been—had not thought to stock his saddlebags with trail grub. No coffee or cornmeal. No salt. Not even any jerky to ease the grumbling in his belly.

But the mail driver would have rations, plenty of them. Plowboys did not drive mail hacks.

Dutch made his decision. With great care, he soaked the bandanna and peeled it off his head. The bandanna was an identifying flag that, for the moment, he did not feel like flying. Wincing, he arranged his hat on his tender head. There was nothing he could do about the saddle rifle and the .45 on his hip, but he made his face as pleasant as possible. Sporting what he hoped was the grin of a carefree cowhand, he touched spurs to the roan and rode across the mail hack's trail.

"Howdy," the murderer hollered, flashing his toothy grin.

"Howdy," the driver responded with no more than normally prudent suspicion.

"Name's Bristow," Dutch said in his most open and friendly manner, glancing at the silent passenger. "Roy Bristow. Comin' from Kansas, makin' for Texas, but I run out of grub about a day out of Caldwell. I aimed on stockin' up in the Outlet, but I'm learnin' that stores down here are mighty spaced out."

The driver laughed dryly. "Stores and people. You're the first live human we've seen all day."

What did he mean by that? Dutch wondered. Had they seen some dead ones?

"Big prairie fire over to the west," the driver explained.

The killer cocked his head and eyed the driver. "Anybody hurt?"

"Must of been. But we didn't see them. Lots of livestock dead in the gullies."

With considerable will power Dutch resisted the temptation to ask about the pitchman. "Prairie fire." He shook his head sorrowfully. "Hard news all around."

The driver grunted. "We aim to stop and cook supper before long. Be proud to have your company, if you feel like stoppin'."

Dutch's instincts told him to take some supplies and go. But there was something in the way the passenger was watching him—a cool, narrow look of suspicion that made Dutch want to know more about him. He was a military man, according to his uniform, although there was nothing military in his bearing. He slouched on the seat beside the driver, his dusty coat unbuttoned, his sidearm swinging from a coat hook behind the seat. There he slouched, heavy-lidded, sulky, saying nothing. But he never moved his gaze from Dutch's face.

"I'm Bo Seward," the driver was saying, warming to the prospect of having somebody to talk to besides the gloomy military man. "I run this hack as a regular thing between Camp Supply and the Katy connection in the Cherokee Nation. This here's Cap'n Still. The cap'n's with the cavalry over at Supply."

"Howdy, Cap'n," Dutch said in the friendliest tone he could manage. "Right proud to meet you."

The captain barely dropped his chin in a moody nod of recognition. *You stuck-up sonofabitch,* Dutch thought to himself. *Don't get fancy with Dutch Rainey, or you'll find yourself meetin' a bullet.* Aloud, he said to the driver, "Much oblige for the invitation. I'd be proud to ride along and take supper with you."

They made camp shortly before sundown, with Dutch pitching in helpfully, unhitching the team, watering and feeding them and putting them out to graze. In the meantime Bo Seward got supper started, while Captain Howard Still walked off a short distance, gazed at the horizon and did nothing. "The bastard's got somethin' on his mind," Dutch thought silently.

The three men ate their side meat and panbread, washing it down with gritty coffee. Seward rambled aimlessly about endless hardships connected with being a hack driver. Dutch listened politely, striving to curb his temper while the captain gazed at him in that dreamy, infuriating way of his.

"I've been wondering," the cavalryman said suddenly, interrupting one of Seward's monotonous monologues. "What is the matter with your head, Mr. Bristow?"

Dutch was startled to discover that he had pushed his hat to one side of his head and was unconsciously clawing at his fiery scalp. He jerked his hand away, as if he had suddenly found it in a fire.

"I mean," the captain went on acidly, "if you want to scratch your head, why don't you remove your hat?"

Dutch's temper soared. "Because it's none of your goddam business!"

Bo Seward looked stunned at his guest's outburst, but Captain Still merely smiled and let his lids droop farther over his eyes. "Curious thing," he mused, as though he were picking up the loose end of a previous discussion. "I heard this morning about a murder over by the Little Arkansas. A sheriff's deputy from Plateau. He was riding a roan gelding like yours at the time. There is some speculation that the killer . . ."

Seward rose to his feet, staring incredulously at his passenger. "Where did you hear such a thing as that?"

"On the telegraph at Pond Creek."

"I didn't hear anything about it."

"The military telegraph. There is some speculation," he continued, "that the killer is a victim of a medicine show pitchman at Plateau. Something to do with a 'hair restorer' which could be very painful to a man with sensitive skin. Fair-skinned persons, that is." He smiled again at Dutch Rainey. "Like you, Mr. Bristow."

Dutch sat cold and rigid, looking at the cavalryman. In his chest he could feel violence bubbling, like a head of warm beer spilling over the rim of a glass. And yet, somehow, he made himself smile. "I don't know what you're talkin' about, Cap'n."

"I think you do, Mr. Rainey."

"Rainey?" Bo Seward blurted. "His name's Bristow."

The captain ignored him. "There's more speculation that you're determined to kill the pitchman when you find him." He smiled his taut, military smile. "Not that you're likely to find him now. Pond Creek's half a day's ride, and you'll never make it, Mr. Rainey."

Dutch observed that the officer was now wearing his official sidearm, a Navy .45, the flap of the holster handily open. But not handy enough, Dutch thought coldly, if there's shootin' to be done.

But there mustn't be any shooting, Dutch warned himself with all the prudence that was in him. He had already allowed his wildness too free a reign. The deputy was dead. The pitchman was dead. There was a limit to how much violent death even a raw new frontier would accept. He gave himself some good advice: *Be smart. Be cool.*

But the cavalryman wouldn't have it. He spoke again, his voice taunting. "Remove your hat, Mr. Rainey. If your head itches, scratch it. It doesn't matter now, your secret is out." As he said it he grabbed for his Navy Colt.

He was surprisingly fast for a military man. Even so, it was Dutch who got off the first shot. The explosion ballooned violently but dissipated almost immediately, absorbed in the leafy growth of liveoak and cottonwood. Captain Howard Still allowed himself a small smile as the bullet struck an iron bracket on the mail hack and went screaming into the darkening sky. Unhurriedly, he fired the heavy Colt.

In shock and pain, Dutch Rainey fell to his knees. The force of the bullet against his rib cage drove the air from his lungs. The world reeled. He saw the captain through a red haze of pain and rage. Still had his revolver held straight out in front of him, at the end of a stiffened arm, like some cool-eyed gentleman from another age who had successfully defended his honor on a dueling plain.

Dutch's only thought at the moment was: *I'm through!* He could feel himself falling forward on his face. He was unable to put out his hands and break the fall. He couldn't even raise his gun hand. He could only wait for the captain to pull the trigger the second time and finish it.

But the captain, for obscure reasons of his own, reasons that Dutch Rainey could never have understood, did not fire a second time. As Dutch fell forward, the officer slowly lowered his Colt. With a little sigh, he said, "Driver, I think he's seriously hurt. You'd better see if there's any medicine in the equipment box." He began to reholster his revolver.

That was his second mistake.

Dutch Rainey, drawing strength from a bottomless well of hate and outrage, managed to drag his gun hand through the gravel. From his position on the ground, he aimed through the campfire. The captain, considering the affair at an end, had turned away and was calling again to the driver.

The bullet struck him in the back of the neck. Howard Still, captain of cavalry, fell like a stone, immediately dead. Dead without pain or shock or realizing what had hit him. This was the only thing about the shot that Dutch found unsatisfactory—that Still had died with so little fuss or pain.

Dutch lay for a long while at the edge of darkness. He could feel the wetness of his own blood, and the streak of fire along his right side. After an eternity of not breathing, as his entire body screamed for air, suddenly his lungs began to function again. For several minutes he gulped the cool air, thinking of nothing else. Then he thought: *Maybe I'm not hurt so bad, after all.*

He tried moving and discovered that it could be done with careful thought and planning. He gathered his strength and called, "Driver, help me!"

There was no sign of the driver. No sound. He had scurried off into the brush at the first sound of shooting. Dutch pulled himself along the ground, leaving a snail-like trail of blood behind him. At last he lay panting beside the dead captain. "You bastard!" he hissed. "I almost wish that second shot had been a little off center so I could have the fun of killin' you again!"

But he realized that wasting energy on futile hatred was foolish. What I've got to do, he thought, is look after this bullet hole in my side and see how bad I'm hurt.

He was gratified to discover that the bullet had merely bounced off his ribs and that most of the damage was in the form of shock and loss of blood. He tore the dead captain's shirt off his body and used it for a bandage. It was slow, painful, and exhausting work, but he did not rest until the wound was bandaged to his satisfaction. He called, "Seward, where the hell are you?"

But the driver was gone. Looking for help, most likely, and that was not a pleasant thing to think about, from Dutch Rainey's point of view. "Help" might well come in the form of angry possemen, or even U. S. Deputy Marshals. "I think," he told himself calmly, "what I better do now is get away from here."

But get away where? With a dead captain of cavalry to his credit, he would no longer find much safety in the Nations. North, toward Kansas, was out of the question, as was Oklahoma Territory to the west.

It was at this point Dutch remembered something the captain had said shortly before he died. *There's speculation that you're determined to kill the pitchman when you find him.* Then the officer had added, *Not that you're likely to find him. Pond Creek's half a day's ride, and you'll never make it . . .*

Was it possible that the pitchman wasn't dead, after all? Had he somehow escaped death in the prairie fire?

The mere thought was enough to send ripples of rage up Dutch's back. After two murders, a dead horse, a bullet in his side, and a twisted knee—after all this, could the pitchman still be alive?

8

YOUNG Hassle Jones was awed and delighted with Oklahoma City. In just five years it had grown from a one-room Santa Fe depot and a few clapboard shacks to a teeming, brawling city that sprawled over the north slope of the Canadian River Valley.

Hassle and California Sam stood on the corner of Broadway and Grand, a lively strip referred to by the natives as Battle Row. "I never seen so many fancy rigs and high-steppin' horses!" the boy said excitedly.

Sam was more interested in the ominous-looking bulges that had mysteriously appeared in men's clothing since a local ordinance had outlawed the carrying of firearms. "She's a lively town, all right, boy. And we got to step lively too, if we aim to have supper tonight, and a place to sleep." He dug all his money out of his pocket and counted it. Allowing for two sandwiches on the train from Pond Creek, they had landed in Oklahoma City with exactly two dollars.

He looked at the money and sighed. "It sure ain't much to work with, but I guess it's got to do."

The first thing the pitchman did was go to a grocery store where, to Hassle's amazement, he spent almost half the bankroll on a large sack of hard candies called "buckshot." Their next visit was to a drugstore; here Sam spent seventy cents on a liberal packet of powdered aloes, and twenty cents' worth of small pillboxes and blank labels. From the druggist he also got a large piece of brown wrapping paper, free of charge.

Their shopping done, they returned to Battle Row where they found a saloon that was empty of customers. Sam spent his last fifteen cents on a large schooner of beer. "It's goin' to be touch and go for a little while," Sam said, as he and the boy took a table in the rear of the saloon. "A ten-minute lecture and a twenty-minute grind, if we're lucky, before the boys in blue bust up the pitch. Well . . ." He spread his hands helplessly. "She can't be helped. We'll have to make the best of a poor situation."

Hassle looked on in fascination as Sam spread the brown paper on the table. Then he emptied the sack of small candy pellets onto the paper, dipped his fingers into the schooner and sprinkled the "buckshot" lightly with beer. Finally he sprinkled the package of powdered aloes over the damp candies and shook the paper until they were thoroughly covered.

"What're you doin'?" Hassle asked at last, when his curiosity could no longer be checked.

"Makin' pills, boy," the pitchman told him impatiently. "What does it look like? You won't find a better pill in any drugstore in the land."

"What's that gray powder you're puttin' on the candy?"

"Powdered aloes, boy. Bitter as sin to a coldwater Baptist. The yokels wouldn't touch it any other way. Besides that, it's a first-class physic, and if there's one thing a yokel insists on in a medicine it's a good workin' out."

California Sam sipped his beer slowly while the pills dried. At last he borrowed a pencil from the bartender, licked the point carefully and began lettering the labels. *WA-HOE INDIAN DYSPEPSIA CURE.* After he had printed several labels he regarded his handiwork objectively. His face grew long with doubt. "I don't know, boy. They don't look very convincin', do they?" But he shrugged his shoulders philosophically. "You got a healthy tongue, boy; start lickin' these labels and stick them on the boxes."

By the time they got the labels lettered and on the boxes, the coating of bitter aloes had dried on the candy buckshot. Sam parceled them out, a dozen to a box. "Well," he sighed at last, "that does it." But there was little enthusiasm in his voice. He sat for some time staring glumly at the stack of little cardboard boxes. "No torches," he said sorrowfully. "It's a sad thing, son, to see a high pitchman commence his lecture without a pair of handsome coal oil torches spittin' fire on either side of him. And not even a rented hack to pitch from! Tell you the truth, boy, I never figgered old California Sam would ever fall quite so low."

Hassle was properly sympathetic. He had heard the medicine man deride low pitchmen, and he suffered with him for now being forced to pitch to the yokels from their own level. The boy's face became stern with thought. "Why don't you ballyhoo outside on the sidewalk, and then make your pitch in here from a table, or even on top of the bar?"

"Boy," the pitchman told him wearily, "you're loco. In the first place, *what* ballyhoo? I haven't even got a rope or deck of cards to do tricks with. In the second place, that bartender ain't goin' to allow no medicine man to pitch from his saloon."

"Why not?" Hassle asked innocently. "I wouldn't mind if *I* was a bartender. If it would bring *customers* into the place."

The pitchman gave the youth a long, hard look. Slowly, his long face began to brighten. "Son, I'm still convinced that one of us is loco, but I'm not so sure any more it's you." He heaved himself out of the chair and lumbered across the room to the deserted bar. "Sir," he told the barkeep in his warmest and friendliest tones, "I've got a business proposition to put to you; I'll lay it out fair and square. What would you say if I told you of a way to fill your saloon with customers?"

The bartender leaned on his mahogany counter and studied the pitchman curiously but without hostility. "I'd say you'd got too much sun. This is the slack time of day, there ain't any customers."

"In that case," Sam reasoned, "you ain't got nothin' to lose. Listen—this is what I've got in mind . . ."

The bartender listened attentively as the medicine man made his pitch. He appreciated a clever swindle as much as the next man—or perhaps it was simply because he was bored with keeping bar in an empty saloon. "I still think you got too much sun. But if you think you can draw customers in the place, you're welcome to try."

Sam turned to Hassle and beamed. "Bring over them pills, boy, we're in business!" To the bartender, he said, "You wouldn't have a deck of cards that I could use, would you? And maybe a few feet of rope that's not too stiff for spinnin'?"

The barkeep obligingly handed over a deck of cards. "There's a rope back in the store room, I think."

Sam went with him to the store room. "And I'll need two beer kegs and a stout plank," he added, riding with his unexpected streak of luck. "Or a couple of good-sized whiskey cases will do, if you ain't got a plank."

Hassle watched with keen appreciation as the pitchman carried two stout whiskey cases out of the saloon and arranged them on the sidewalk. With the blissful air of a man who had just escaped a fate worse than death, he stepped upon the whiskey cases. California Sam—even without torches and other flash—was still the high pitchman. He had not compromised himself by pitching to the yokels on their own level.

The medicine man produced the borrowed deck of cards and announced loudly to no one at all, "Gentlemen, if you'll just step a little closer, I will show you something to tantalize and mystify and amaze you! In my hands you see a common deck of cards. An ordinary deck of cards, my friends. Now watch closely." He fanned the cards with the expertise of a New Orleans monte dealer. Four aces popped into the air. He fanned the cards a second time and four kings shot out.

"Watch closely now," the pitchman warned happily, as though he were addressing a crowded auditorium. He showered the cards from hand to hand. He shuffled the cards with great flare. Then he dealt himself a royal flush.

Across the street a pair of cowhands came out of a saloon. They stopped for a moment, gaping at the odd-looking bird standing on the whiskey cases and flipping cards into the air. After a while they came across the street to see what he was up to.

"Ah!" Sam beamed at them, all the while shuffling the cards, fanning them and producing a straight flush. The card trick did not seem to impress them, so the medicine man turned and gestured dramatically to Hassle. "Now, gentlemen, if my young assistant will be so kind . . ."

Hassle was so kind as to hand him the length of worn hemp rope that he had borrowed from the bartender. A passing drummer paused and lit a cigar and waited to see what he was going to do with the rope. Before long the two cowhands and the drummer were joined by a townsman, a railroad brakeman, and an iceman. "There you are, gentlemen, a common, ordinary hemp rope. Step just a little closer, please. Folks behind you want to see, too." He shook out a small loop and began spinning it.

A delighted Hassle stood in the saloon doorway with the barkeep, watching a crowd gather as if by magic. The hemp loop grew and shrunk, dipped and looped, formed figure eights, ocean waves, sailed out in flat little whirring arcs. It stood on end as a hempen doorway for the pitchman to step through, first with one foot and then with the other. The cowhands, who worked with ropes as naturally as they worked with their hands, stared open-mouthed at the fantastically performing loop. The crowd grew slowly but steadily. When there were perhaps thirty men crowded in front of the saloon the pitchman shot a meaningful look at Hassle.

Hassle understood that the medicine man's ballyhoo time had expired. It was now time to move inside the saloon where he could hopefully deliver a brief pitch and grind before the police had a chance to interfere.

California Sam formed one last gigantic loop, lifted it high in the air and let it fall around his body with a flourish. Impulsively, a few of the more innocent yokels clapped their hands in appreciation. The pitchman fairly stunned them with the brilliance of his smile. "Thank you, thank you, gentlemen! That was only the beginnin' of our show! The best is yet to come, and it's all free, gentlemen, every bit of it, absolutely free! If you'll just step inside the saloon where we'll be more comfortable, the show will get underway immediately!"

To the bartender's amazement, the crowd actually began to move toward the saloon entrance. Alertly, he and Hassle opened wide the swinging doors, while California Sam intoned, "That's right, gentlemen, move right inside. Make yourself comfortable." He eyed them with a wolfish grin. "You might even want to have a little go at the bartender's wares!"

To the barkeep's further amazement, several grinning yokels found the pitchman's suggestion a perfectly agreeable one. They rested their feet comfortably on the brass rail and put in their orders. As soon as the commotion had settled down and the bartender had happily collected on his sales, California Sam climbed, with considerable grunting, to the top of the bar.

The yokels cocked their heads in vague surprise as they looked up at him. This was the same pitchman they had seen outside, doing card tricks and spinning rope like a headliner at the opera house—but at the same time he was different. The man who looked down at them clearly had deep and disturbing thoughts in his mind. "Gentlemen," he addressed them gravely, "I know I promised you another show in here, and California Sam always keeps his promises. But, with your kind permission, I'd like to be serious for just a minute."

The yokels mentally shrugged their permission for him to do as he pleased. Some of them motioned the bartender for another round.

"Gentlemen," California Sam began, "I want to tell you a story. A true story, mind you . . ."

A grinning Hassle Jones lounged against the far end of the bar and listened to the pitchman change moods as smoothly as a blooded pacer changing gaits. He launched into his tale of the young white hunter trespassing on the homeland of the savage Wa-Hoe Indians. The natives listened open-mouthed as California Sam dramatically rescued young San-To, only son of Ho-Wa-Wa, chief of all the Wa-Hoes. With a mind to the passage of time, Sam shortened his lecture by more than half, but the yokels were thoroughly hooked by the time he got around to describing the miraculous cures that he had witnessed at the hands of the Wa-Hoe medicine men—all due, of course, to the magic ingredients of a small gray pellet that the pitchman had named Wa-Hoe Indian Dyspepsia Cure.

"Gentlemen," California Sam assured his audience, "there ain't hardly any sickness known to medical science that these little pills won't cure. If there is a disease that they won't cure outright, why they'll make the patient feel so good that pretty soon he'll forget what it was he had in the first place. Upset stomach, achin' back, sore muscles, kidney trouble, or general debility. I seen them medicine men cure them all with them little gray pellets. Well, you can imagine that I took a keen interest in the way the Wa-Hoe medicine men treated their patients. I was amazed, gentlemen, amazed, at the way them innocent-lookin' little pellets could, by immediately improvin' the patient's general health, completely change the way he looked and felt. Why, gentlemen, I've seen old Wa-Hoe warriors that looked well on the road to the dyin' ground, and after a few of these little pills their eyes would clear, their skin would take on the glow of youth, and almost all their wrinkles would disappear. Their hair would stop fallin' out, and they would step out with pride and vigor like young men!"

Hassle, from his position at the end of the bar, kept a close eye on the pitchman. When he got the signal he quickly moved up the polished mahogany with the stack of small boxes.

"Well, gentlemen," Sam wound up his pitch, "you can imagine how overwhelmed I was when Ho-Wa-Wa, the old chief of the Wa-Hoes, directed his head medicine man to reveal to me the secret of those little magic pellets, on account of the way I had saved his boy for him . . ."

Hassle was aware that the pitch, having been edited rather drastically, had lost a good deal of its dramatic impact. But the yokels didn't seem to notice.

"Gentlemen," California Sam was saying, his voice trembling slightly with the import of his words, "I have with me today a few boxes of those little pellets. The name that the Wa-Hoes have for them is not translatable into our language; I call them Wa-Hoe Indian Dyspepsia Cure, but you gentlemen may well call them pure magic after you've tried them. I see what you're thinkin', sir!" he exclaimed to one startled native, fixing him for a moment with a watery eye. "You're thinkin' these lettle pellets must cost a fortune! A king's ransom!"

With the skill of a Booth, the pitchman's voice slid down the scale and struck the perfect note of awe and wonderment. "Well, sir, you would be perfectly justified in thinkin' just that! Any sensitive, intelligent person would think exactly what you're thinkin' at this minute. And yet . . ." He paused for further drama. "And *yet,* you're absolutely wrong, sir! These wonderful little pellets do not sell for one hundred dollars a box, as you might well imagine. They do not sell for fifty dollars a box." He closed his eyes for a moment, clearly shaken by what he was about to say. "Gentlemen, this wonderful Wa-Hoe Indian Dyspepsia Cure does not sell for even *ten* dollars a box! And for a very simple reason. On the day I left the homeland of the savage Wa-Hoe Indians, I promised old Ho-Wa-Wa and his head medicine man that I would use the secret of these little pellets for the benefit of mankind. I gave them my word of honor! And that precisely is the reason these pellets do not cost a fortune in diamonds and rubies, as any sensible man might expect. I know you're goin' to find this hard to believe. But on that day when I left the mountains of the Wa-Hoes I promised—I gave my word—that I would never sell these pellets for more than a dollar a box! And that," he added, slightly dazed with the brightness of his own nobility, "is exactly what I'm doin' today, gentlemen. No man among you will pay more than a single dollar for a box of this magical Dyspepsia Cure—because California Sam is a man of his word!"

Quickly, Hassle shoved the neat pile of pillboxes under the feet of the pitchman. Sam shot a quick glance at the saloon's swinging doors, then turned quickly to a startled yokel and smiled benignly. "Ah, I see this gentleman wants to make the first purchase today. I must say it speaks well for your alertness and intelligence, sir!"

Sam reached out and thrust the pillbox into the sucker's hand. Before the yokel fully realized what had happened, the pitchman had relieved him of a dollar bill. Several of the natives looked slightly stunned, due largely to the force of the lecture and the obliging bartender. Yes, California Sam thought happily as he accepted another dollar bill, I ought to of thought of pitchin' in a saloon myself! That boy's got the makin's of a first-class medicine man in him!

The pitchman shoved several of the pillboxes into Hassle's hands. "Make your change directly after a sale," he instructed from the side of his mouth. "Don't make another sale until you know the change is right."

Hassle plunged into the crowd waving a pillbox over his head. Someone thrust a five-dollar bill into his hand. Following the pitchman's instructions, he got the bartender to break the bill and gave the yokel his change before trying for another sale. The excitement of making sales and changing money, was a heady experience to the youth. For the first time in his life he felt important and in the thick of things, not a young nobody who cleaned stalls for the privilege of sleeping in a barn loft.

Still in his position as high pitchman on the bar, California Sam had gone automatically into his grind. "There you are, sir. One silver dollar; that's right, sir." He made change with the same flourish that he produced four straight aces from a poker deck, all the while keeping up a hypnotic flow of words.

"Almost daily," he assured the yokels, "some happy soul comes up to me and wants to shake my hand for introducin' him to Wa-Hoe Indian Dyspepsia Cure. Only yesterday a fine-lookin', well-dressed man stopped me on the street of this very city. He said, 'Doctor, you won't remember me, but I am the poor, run-down wretch that listened to your lecture on the street of Denver just a year ago. I was so run-down, my body so weak from a bad stomach and a general debility of the system that I couldn't hold a job. My good wife had to go back to her folks in Kansas and take the children with her. My life was hell, sir, and I could see no way out. Then, when I had almost given up all hope,

I chanced to hear your lecture about the noble Wa-Hoe medicine men and the miraculous cures they achieved through the use of secret herbs and chemical formulas. Well, sir, I purchased a box of Wa-Hoe Indian Dyspepsia Cure from you that day, and I now stand before you a changed man. A *changed man*, sir. My dear wife and children are back with me; I am employed as a head teller in the First National Bank, and I am proud to say that I am again a respected member of society and the Methodist Church.' One silver dollar, sir. Thank you!"

The pitchman's reserve of Wa-Hoe Indian Dyspepsia Cure had been reduced to just three boxes when the swinging doors flew inward and a rumpled, world-weary policeman bellowed, "You're under arrest! Don't you know that sellin' medicine without a license is against the law?"

The pitchman put on a face of shocked innocence. "I never knowed anything of the kind, officer. Do I look like the kind of man that would deliberately set out to break the law?" As smoothly as a poker shark would slip a fifth ace into a deck, he passed his newly acquired currency into the surprised hand of Hassle Jones. Climbing down from the bar, he approached the policeman with a fatherly smile. "Sir, I give you my word that I never heard anything whatsoever about a license to sell medicine. I assure you that I'll straighten the matter up just as soon as . . ."

"Tell it to the judge," the policeman told him sourly. He sized the pitchman up with a jaded eye. "I ain't goin' to have to cuff you, am I?"

"Sir," said California Sam indignantly, "I assure you . . ."

"All right," the lawman shrugged, "follow me."

The crowd of yokels grinned self-consciously, most of them clutching boxes of Wa-Hoe Indian Dyspepsia Cure, as the policeman led the medicine man out of the saloon and up the street. As he went through the swinging doors, the pitchman grinned and winked at his young assistant. Hassle grinned and winked back.

About an hour after his arrest a guard came back to the pitchman's cell in Oklahoma City's Cottonwood d'Bastille —as the native wits called their city prison—and unlocked the barred door. He was shown into a dreary, dank-smelling room which might have served as a model for all police courts in the country. A beefy Irish sergeant was glaring at a tearful Hassle Jones.

California Sam—who had an extraordinary sensitivity to such things—did not sense any hostility in the room. Hassle's tears and youthful pleading had obviously softened this roomful of stony police hearts. The pitchman's chest swelled with pride. The boy was learning well!

The police judge fixed his little bullet eyes on Sam. "Are you the medicine pitchman known as California Sam?"

Sam confessed that he was.

"If you're a pitchman," the judge said sternly, "you know all about peddler's licenses. But because this is your first offense, and because of the boy's eloquent plea in your behalf, I'm lettin' you off with a warnin' this time."

Sam beamed happily.

"And," the judge added with a grim little smile, "a ten-dollar fine."

Sam's wide smile slipped a bit, but he was still cheerful. He understood perfectly what was happening. Police hearts might have been melted by Hassle's tears, but the judge was all business. The fine was to let the pitchman know that the next time he would not be so lucky.

Hassle and the pitchman stood on Battle Row, at the corner of West Grand and Broadway, admiring the way the city came to life when the sun went down. Sam rubbed his hands together happily. In his pocket was twenty-two dollars left over from the Dyspepsia Cure pitch. He was itching to start another pitch, a real pitch this time, on a busy corner, from the back of a stylish hack.

"How much does a license cost?" Hassle asked.

"Maybe fifty dollars." Sam shrugged. "But only suckers buy licenses. Tomorrow I'll scout around and make a fix, but right now we better look for a place to stay."

"I'm hungry," Hassle said.

"I swear, boy, it seems like you're always hungry." Sam grinned and patted his head. "But that's all right, you earned yourself a steak dinner today in that courtroom." He chuckled to himself. "I swear, when the guard brought me in from the cell you had that bunch of harness bulls ready to bust out in tears."

Hassle grinned and puffed a little with pride. "Are you goin' to pitch again tonight?"

"Can't pitch again till I make a fix. The next arrest will mean six months on the work gang—and that ain't no picnic excursion to St. Louis."

They found the Southern Hotel on North Broadway near the Santa Fe tracks. The two-story house, with outside stairway, sat forlornly behind a picket fence, in a jungle of climbing roses and weeds. A scaling sign on the front gallery announced: ROOM AND BOARD $1.

"Well," Sam sighed, "it ain't the Palace Hotel in San Francisco, but the price is right."

A hatchet-faced woman with the voice of a muleskinner looked faintly startled to see them. "You're late for supper." Suddenly she grinned like a Charleston gambler who had just won the deal. "But that's all right. Take a chair, make yourself comfortable." She disappeared through a pair of swinging doors to the kitchen and for a time there was a busy rattle of pots and pans.

Hassle looked up at the pitchman. "You said a steak dinner."

"I know what I said, boy. And I meant it . . . Tomorrow. Right now there's more important things to do with our money. Like buyin' torches, and rentin' a hack, and fixin' the town."

They sat at a long plank table while the landlady—a widow by the name of Hattie Brent—brought in the food. "There you are, gents, dig in. There's plenty more where this come from."

They sat for several minutes staring at the heaping platters. Boiled potatoes cooked to a soupy gruel, turnips floating in a sea of greenish liquid, great slabs of fat meat stranded on shoals of congealed grease, biscuits as hard as a lumberjack's fist. The pitchman looked at Hassle with his watery eyes. "Maybe," he said without much hope, "it ain't as bad as it looks."

But it was. They ate enough to still the grumbling in their bellies, then paid the landlady for a night's lodging. "Didn't like it much, did you?" Mrs. Hattie Brent asked with a wry grin. "Can't say as I blame you. My late husband, Mr. Brent, always said my cookin' was the worst he'd et anywhere west of Kansas City. Well, the rooms are clean, anyhow. And you don't have to eat the grub if you don't want it."

As Mrs. Brent had promised, the room was small but antiseptically clean. There was an oak bunk, a trundle bed for Hassle, a washstand and a wardrobe, everything polished to a fine luster by years of rubbing and dusting. Hassle leaned out of the window, his eyes shining with excitement. "Let's go out and look at the town," he begged. "It wouldn't cost nothin' to do that, would it?"

"Time is money," the pitchman said mysteriously. "Right now we got better ways to spend our time than walkin' the streets like a pair of yokels. Set down now and pay attention. I'm goin' to learn you mind readin'."

Hassle turned from the window, blinking. "Learn me what?"

"Mind readin', boy. Is there somethin' the matter with your hearin'?" He dug in his pocket and found a stub of a pencil and some scrap paper. His long face folded in deep furrows of thought, he began writing on the paper. "Maybe I'm mistaken," he said, the pencil moving steadily, "but I kind of had the feelin' that you wanted to take part in the pitch tomorrow."

"Well, sure," Hassle told him. "I want to help. But I can't read nobody's mind."

"Nobody can, but the yokels don't know that. By the time I get through with you we'll have the suckers convinced that you can look right through their thick skulls and see their thoughts, like watchin' goldfish in a glass bowl. Here, can you read this?"

It was a list of common articles that might be found in any crowd. Hat, stickpin, boots, necktie . . . "I can read it," the boy told him.

"Fine, fine! All right, here's what we've got, a mind readin' code based on the alphabet. The simplest piece of ballyhoo known to man. But, if it's done right, the yokels never catch on. Are you ready?"

"For what?"

"To learn that list, what did you think? Start at the top. 'A' is hat. 'B' is stickpin. 'C' is boots. See what I mean?"

Hassle nodded doubtfully. "I think so."

"All right, get busy and learn the list." He smiled brightly, then reached for his hat and walked out of the room.

In an hour he was back, smoking a new corncob pipe and smelling of Kentucky bourbon. "You got that code in your mind now?"

"I got it in my mind," Hassle told him, "but I don't see what it's got to do with mind readin'."

"Patience, boy. You got to learn patience." The pitchman took the list and studied it for a moment to refresh his memory. "This," he said briskly, "is what we'll do. First we'll ride up and down the street in the hack, and I'll holler to the natives that we're about to give them a free show. Then we'll stop on the best corner in town, Broadway and Grand, right across from City Hall. That's where we'll make our pitch."

"How're you goin' to pitch without a license?"

"Didn't I tell you, boy?" the medicine man asked in astonishment. "I just made the fix. The go-between's a bartender at a place called the Day and Night Saloon. Cost me twenty dollars, but the corner's worth it. The go-between'll keep five for hisself and scatter the rest amongst the police judge and the harness bulls on the beat. There's nothin' to worry about. We don't need a license. Anyhow," he went on, picking up the thread of his thought, "we stop there at the corner of Broadway and Grand, unhitch and light our torches, and that's where we'll make our pitch."

"What are you goin' to sell this time?"

"I ain't made up my mind yet—maybe the Wa-Hoe Indian Herb Mixture. It depends on whether I can locate a wholesale drug outfit and what kind of bargain I can make for a batch of herbs. Stop interruptin' me. There we are on the corner. I make a little spiel and get a crowd of natives around the hack. Then I'll look real serious for a minute and start somethin' like this: Gentlemen, I want you to look at this young boy sittin' here beside me in this carriage. A fine-lookin', clean-cut lad, you say to yourselves, but he looks pretty much like any other boy his age. What's so different about him that I ought to stand here lookin' at him? Well, gentlemen, what I am about to tell you you're goin' to find hard to believe. But it's the Lord's truth—you have the word of California Sam on it. What's more, I aim to prove it to the satisfaction of the most cynical man in this fair city. Gentlemen, this young lad you're lookin' at right this minute possesses the rarest gift in all of God's creation! *This boy is a reader of minds!*"

Hassle stared at him. "You talkin' about *me*?"

"'Course, I'm talkin' about you boy. As soon as I figger the crowd's ready, I'll wind up the spiel and we'll give them a demonstration. First, I'll blindfold you. Or, better, have one of the yokels come up and do it. Then I'll circulate amongst the suckers, and pretty soon I'll holler, 'What is this, my lad? What is this item I'm touchin' with my hand?' What do you say to that?"

Hassle thought furiously. His mind went to the first item on the list. "Hat!" he blurted. "It's a hat!"

"Correct," the medicine man beamed. "Now give me the name of *this* item, if you will."

"Stickpin!" Hassle shot back immediately.

"Fine," the pitchman told him with fatherly pride. "But not quite so fast. Don't make it look too easy. Now, gentlemen, let us see if the boy can name this item I'm now pointin' to."

"It . . ." Hassle hesitated, frowning thoughtfully. "It's *two* items."

"Oh?" California Sam raised one shaggy eyebrow. "How is that?"

"You're pointin' to a pair of boots."

"Very good," Sam told him with controlled admiration. He put a fatherly hand on the boy's shoulder. "Yes, sir, I do believe you have the makin's of a pitchman!"

The next day was a busy one for the medicine man and the young mind reader. Sam found a wholesale druggist with initiative and imagination and arranged for a shipment of mixed herbs on a plan of deferred payment—at elevated prices—after offering evidence that he had already arranged a fix with the city go-between. In more or less the same way he made arrangements with a tinsmith to construct a pair of coal oil torches, and with a printer for five hundred herb mixture labels. Finally, he arranged for the rental of a handsome red-trimmed barouche and two high-stepping blacks.

"There she is, boy," he told Hassle with a sigh. "The rest is up to us, and the bilious livers of the natives."

On the stroke of seven that night Sam drove the barouche out of the wagon yard on lower Broadway. Hassle Jones sat rigidly beside him, his face a little paler than usual. From time to time he would gulp spasmodically and his Adam's apple would bob up and down like a button on a string.

"Feelin' a little skitterish?" the pitchman asked cheerfully.

"I'm feelin' fine," Hassle told him weakly.

"Well, don't fret about it if you do. Some of the best bally-hoo men I ever seen couldn't hardly call their names the first time they faced a pack of yokels. You'll get over it."

"When the time comes, what if I can't recollect that list?"

"You will."

"But what if I can't?"

"The world won't come to an end, boy. That's somethin' to remember. No matter how bad a pitch goes, there's always tomorrow."

The boy heaved an enormous sigh, but not of relief. His mind was racing like mice in a spinning wheel. He could recite that list forward and backward and inside-out, and yet he knew beyond the faintest doubt that he would not remember a single word of it when the time came.

"Sam," he blurted as they crossed California Street, "I can't do it!"

"Sure you can," the pitchman told him comfortably. "Any-how, you can try. That's all a body can ask."

"I'll ruin your pitch."

"Remember what I told you. There's always tomorrow and another pitch. Gentle down, boy, you're spooky as a green bronc in the springtime."

Hassle eyed the medicine man with passionate envy. California Sam sat smiling serenely, nodding to surprised natives as the blacks pranced gracefully toward the hub corner of Broadway and Grand. When they reached the corner the pitchman applied the brake, stood up in the hack, made a formal little bow. Suddenly he hollered in a bull-like voice to a startled group of cowhands standing in front of a saloon. "Free show, gentlemen! Free show to-night! Commences in just a few minutes, an amazing demonstration of mind readin'!"

Still standing, he turned the team in the middle of the street and headed back south. "Free show commences in just a few minutes!" he hollered again at a cluster of loitering townsmen. "At the corner of Broadway and Grand, gents! Free show! Free show!"

The pitchman thrust the lines into Hassle's hands without missing a beat in his foghorn harangue. They returned to California Street, where Hassle, with considerable sweating, hauled the blacks around. Finally they came to a lurching halt directly across the street from City Hall, in front of a cluster of saloons and second-floor gambling halls. Saloon women in gaudy dresses and rouged faces draped themselves in open windows, waving and laughing at the pitchman, exchanging raucous jokes with the natives.

Standing on the driver's seat, California Sam beamed down at them. Even in his bedraggled condition he was the perfect picture of a high pitchman. One of the natives volunteered to unhitch the team and help Hassle lash the torches to the front wheels. In less than five minutes the torches were lighted and Sam went into his pitch.

Hassle sat stiffly on the front-facing seat of the barouche, trying to look unconcerned. But his thoughts whirled at a dizzying rate. His hands trembled. He was sweating so much that his unruly hair was soon plastered to his forehead. His stomach felt as if it had shriveled to the size of a pea and was hiding somewhere behind his liver. The cold grip of panic had taken hold of him.

Appalled, he watched California Sam climbing out of the hack and realized that the introductory spiel was over and the time for the actual demonstration had arrived. A hundred wild thoughts crashed in the youth's mind. I'll jump out of this hack and run and run and run and they'll never catch me! I'll throw myself under a dray wagon and kill myself!

Stunned, he watched one of the grinning townsmen climbing up on the running board of the hack. Hassle lurched to his feet and looked around wildly. There was no escape. Yokels completely encircled the hack, like hostile

Comanches circling a wagon train. They know I'm tryin' to make a fool of them, he thought hopelessly. I'm done for!

But the man seemed to be grinning without hostility. He whipped out a large red bandanna and, before Hassle could move, tied it securely over the boy's eyes. Hassle heard California Sam calling from the audience: "My boy, please tell these good folks what it is I'm now touchin' with my finger."

Hat, Hassle thought numbly. "A" on the list. The first item of the code. An icy rivulet of sweat streaked down his back. "Hat!" he blurted almost in hysteria.

There was a good-natured murmur from the crowd. Hassle stood frozen, waiting for the sky to fall. But all that happened was California Sam calling cheerfully, "That's exactly correct, my boy. Now don't rush yourself. Concentrate. Take as long as you like." The pitchman moved through the crowd until he found a man wearing a necktie with a small cameo stickpin. With the sucker's dazzled permission, he touched the stickpin lightly with his finger. "What item am I touchin' now?"

"Stickpin!" Hassle shot back automatically.

The crowd murmured again. From that moment Hassle realized that the suckers were not actually his enemies. They were going along with childlike innocence with the mind-reading act. They were entertained because they wanted to be entertained. Or, as California Sam would have said, a sucker never questioned anything he thought was free, and they were still under the impression that this was a free show.

The mind-reading act wound up an unqualified triumph. The yokels clapped their hands and whistled when the pitchman finally climbed back into the hack and whipped the blindfold away from Hassle's eyes.

The rest of the night, as far as Hassle Jones was concerned, passed in a rosy haze. He had never been applauded before—it was a heady experience. He had never imagined a sea of faces staring up at him with respect or something very like it. He felt dazed and drunk with his own importance. He had a crazy urge to jump out of the hack and start collaring natives and explain to them that he was Hassle Jones—*the* Hassle Jones—the eleven-year-old boy who could read men's minds!

California Sam was well into his Herb Mixture pitch, dramatically rescuing the son of Ho-Wa-Wa and winning the flinty hearts of the savage Wa-Hoe Indians. Hassle heard none of it. He sat dazzled by his own brilliance. After what could have been minutes or hours he was startled to have the pitchman loading his arms with boxes of mixed herbs.

"Remember now, make your change for one sale before you start goin' after another one."

California Sam slipped effortlessly into his grind while making sales out of the hack. Hassle circulated in the crowd, placing boxes of herb mixture into eager yokel hands, making change.

"One dollar. That's correct. Thank you, sir."

Then, like a curtain falling at the end of an exciting stage play, it was all over. Sam and Hassle put out the torches and stowed them in back of the rented hack. They hitched the team and drove back to the wagon yard.

"Well, boy," Sam asked happily, "what do you think?"

Hassle, still in something of a daze, shook his head slowly. "I don't know. It's different from what I thought it would be. After ever'thing got goin', it was kind of . . ."

"Excitin'?"

The boy nodded. "I guess that's it."

The pitchman laughed. "I seen it. After you got past the hat and stickpin you had them natives eatin' out of your hand. You got natural flash, boy—to a pitchman that's better'n a license to steal."

Hassle shot him a curious look. "You think I'll ever make a pitchman? A real pitchman, I mean, like you?"

"I'd stake my reputation on it, boy. What do you say we rustle up a steak dinner after we get this hack back to the barn?"

It was a little past midnight when they found the railroad cafe near the Santa Fe depot. The steak was tough and stringy; the fried potatoes had been cooked that afternoon and were as hard as poker chips—it was the best meal that Hassle Jones had ever tasted.

For one thing, this was the first time he had ever eaten a real meal at this hour of the night. He sat with the pitchman in a plank booth, still absorbing and digesting the excitement of the night. A great variety of customers frequented the cafe, it seemed. Railroad signalmen, early passengers waiting for trains that were late, cowhands, and just plain loafers. Once a woman in a red dress and painted lips came in and joined the cook. Nobody seemed to think it strange that an eleven-year-old boy should be eating his big meal of the day at one o'clock in the morning.

California Sam shot him a crooked grin. "You're feelin' pretty good, ain't you?"

"Sure, I guess so."

"Just because you fooled the yokels tonight, don't start thinkin' you got a real mind-readin' act."

"What do you mean?"

"A real act takes a lot of time and a lot of work. Take the first item in the alphabet code—'A' for hat. A real ballyhoo man would break that down a dozen ways. What kind of hat is it? Is it a derby, a bowler, a straw hat, a sombrero, or what? Maybe it's not even a hat at all but a cap. What color is it? Black, blue, brown, white? There has to be a code for everything, or pretty soon the suckers begin to catch on. Then you're finished."

Hassle was not in the least dismayed. He rested secure

in the conviction that there was nothing that he could not do—absolutely nothing—if he put his mind to it. And if he had a little help from California Sam. "I don't mind workin' on it."

"Good, because you got to learn a whole new set of code words before the next pitch."

"I'll learn them. How much money did we make tonight?"

"Boy, sometimes I think the only things that go through your mind are eatin' and money."

"How much?"

The pitchman dug into his pocket and thumbed through a roll of greenbacks. He looked up with a pleased grin. "Not bad, considerin'. Seventy dollars in paper."

"How much silver?"

"One thing you got to learn, boy," Sam told him sternly. "The world is full of robbers and thieves. Only fools flash their money in public places. We'll count it when we get back to Mrs. Brent's."

"What do you aim to do with all that money?"

"For one thing, we'll go out tomorrow and buy ourselves some fancy duds. Clothes make the man. That ain't always true, but a good part of the time it is. Then we'll settle up with the druggist and the printer and the tinsmith. Also, I got an uneasy feelin' that the city go-between will be lookin' us up tomorrow wantin' another fix."

The boy looked at him steadily. "After you do all them things, you'll be clear to pitch every day, won't you?"

"I don't see why not."

"Then what do you aim to do with the money you make?"

Sam regarded his assistant with a slightly jaded eye. "Boy," he said sorrowfully, "there's one more thing you got to learn, if you aim to get along in this world. You got to learn to trust your partner."

Hassle thought about that for a time and decided to let the matter drop. For the moment it was enough that California Sam had started thinking of him as a partner.

9

A LONG time ago—it seemed like half a lifetime, with the blazing bullet wound in his side and a twisted knee to remind him—a long time ago, Dutch Rainey decided definitely that he would not be going to the Cherokee Nation after all. The dead captain of cavalry had said—or at least implied—that the medicine show pitchman had made it to Pond Creek. That thought bored into Dutch's brain like a beetle boring into a sandhill. *The pitchman was still alive and in Pond Creek.* Therefore, Dutch would go to Pond Creek. No other thought occurred to him.

Flying in the face of all reason—for he was now a driven man and deaf to reason—Dutch put his jaded roan over the seemingly endless expanse of brown prairie. His saddle wet with his own blood, his knee swollen and stiff, he managed by scant seconds to avoid one military posse from Supply. Closer to Pond Creek he hid in a gully for an hour as a sheriff's posse of cowhands and farmers beat the brush of a creek bottom.

The military posse told him that someone had found the dead captain. The mail driver had probably made his way to some settlement, and from there to a telegraph. That meant that half the settlers in the Territory would know about him and be looking for him. But that didn't change anything; it only made him regret missing the chance to kill the driver while he was at it. If he realized that he was a doomed man he did not dwell on it. The pitchman was also doomed. That was the important thing.

With the luck of those who are blind to danger, Dutch Rainey rode untouched into Pond Creek in the early afternoon, slightly less than twenty hours after killing the cavalry officer. Where he might find the pitchman, he had no notion. But he knew where to find someone who would know.

He limped into the Rock Island depot as the operator was chalking a change of time for the southbound. To El Reno. With a face as gray as death, his eyes burning, he drew his .45 while the operator's back was still turned. He said hoarsely, "Where's the pitchman?"

Lloyd Toom, the railroad's representative in Pond Creek, felt his stomach dive. From the messages on the telegraph he knew all about Dutch Rainey's insane vendetta. But with military posses and sheriff's posses sweeping the prairie, it didn't seem possible that the killer could have evaded all of them.

But he had, somehow. There was no doubt about that.

"The pitchman," Dutch snarled again, drilling the muzzle of his revolver into the operator's back. He grabbed Toom's shoulder and wheeled him around. "You got just about as much time as it takes this hammer to fall to tell me."

The operator made a strangling sound in his throat. Violence and death radiated from Dutch Rainey like heat waves from a summer desert. "He ain't here," Toom managed in a panic. "Him and the boy's in Oklahoma City."

"What boy?"

"The one that caused all the trouble. I forget his name. And last night the woman left too. Her name is Rose McGee."

"Ahhh," Dutch sighed softly, as if the name had some profound meaning for him. "I want to know all about the pitchman and the boy and the woman called Rose McGee!"

Under the hypnotic fascination of the cocked revolver, Toom blurted every detail that he could think of that might possibly interest the killer.

Dutch absorbed it all with the same slack, death mask expression. With a long, aching sigh he sank onto the depot bench. He tried not to think of the knifelike pain in his side or the throbbing of his knee. He had to make up his mind what to do about the operator.

"Where is everybody?" he asked at last. "The town's dead. Nobody in the street."

"They're out lookin' for you," the operator told him nervously.

Dutch's mask cracked in a small, grim smile. All of his instincts urged him to kill the operator, but he didn't want to risk rousing the town with a shot. If he was to make Oklahoma City, he would need all the head start he could get. "Turn around," he said.

Lloyd Toom's haggard face went chalky white. "Don't kill me, mister," he begged in a quivering voice. "Please don't kill me."

"Turn around," Dutch told him with his death mask grin.

The operator did as he was told. Dutch, with furious determination, pushed himself up off the bench. He lifted the .45 and swung with all his might at the back of Toom's head.

Even so, it was not a death blow, and Dutch Rainey knew it. He was too weak, too fluttery with exhaustion, to kill with his hands. To hell with you, he thought coldly. You can't stop me now. Nobody can. He reeled into the cubicle behind the ticket window and tried to rip the telegraph receiver loose from the wiring. He sagged against the wall, gasping for breath. I could shoot it to pieces, he thought. But he still didn't want to call attention to himself with a shot. He had gone through too much to get his hands on that pitchman, he was not going to spoil it now. "To hell with you," he said aloud to the operator's still form on the floor.

He made his way slowly out of the depot. With an almost inaudible little scream he got his foot in the stirrup and hauled himself up to the saddle. Then, without a backward look, he rode south.

It was their third night of pitching on the corner of Broadway and Grand. California Sam glowed with good cheer and fine Kentucky bourbon. The pitch was exceeding his fondest expectations; Hassle was hard at work learning a complicated code for the mind-reading act, and the natives were all but forcing their money into their pockets. "Boy," California Sam told his assistant happily, "when you feel Lady Luck runnin' with you, the way I feel her now, it's downright bull-headedness not to do somethin' about it."

"Like what?" Hassle asked, stowing the torches in the back of their rented barouche.

"Like poker, son. We got us a nice little bankroll; it seems a shame not to invest it in a sure thing."

"I never heard that poker was such a sure thing."

"All depends in how you play it, boy."

A ripple of uneasiness went up Hassle's back. More than once he had been amazed at the pitchman's skill at manipulating a deck of cards, but he wasn't at all sure that professional gamblers would be so impressed. "I saw a cowhand once at the Western Trail in Wichita," he said offhandedly. "He could turn a deck inside out and put it together again before you could hardly see it."

"Matter of practice," Sam told him comfortably.

"He was the best I ever seen, until I seen you. I don't guess you knew him. His name was Slick Potter."

"I don't think I ever had the honor."

"Well, one night at the Western Trail a visitin' gambler from Caldwell decided to count the deck. There wasn't but three aces in it."

Sam shot him a slanted look. "You tryin' to tell me somethin', boy?"

"They found the missin' ace in a little hold-out that Slick had strapped to his arm under his sleeve. The man from Caldwell's name was Ben Struther."

"Go on, boy," the pitchman said.

"That's all there is to it. Ben Struther shot Slick through his left vest pocket. I just thought I'd mention it."

"Proud you did," Sam told him heartily. "If I ever play cards with a gent called Struther I'll be careful not to wear a hold-out."

From the wagon yard they strolled east on Grand, along that noisy stretch of saloons and gambling halls known as Bunco Alley. Sam paused in front of a place called the Lucky Frisco. He took this as a good omen, for San Francisco was considered a pitchman's paradise. "Son," he said, dropping a few silver coins into Hassle's hand, "you go on down to that railroad cafe and fill up on grub. I aim to try my luck."

"How long will you be?"

"That depends on how much money's in the game, and how stubborn the other players are."

The pitchman, splendid once again in a new rig of buckskins, disappeared through the swinging doors of the saloon. Hassle continued on toward the Santa Fe tracks, alertly skipping out of the way of reeling drunks, grinning up at the painted ladies who lounged sleepily in upstairs windows.

"Howdy, boy," the counterman said as Hassle sauntered into the cafe. "Where's the old doc tonight?"

"Stopped off at the Lucky Frisco. I'll have the usual."

The counterman prepared the boy's nightly order of steak and fried potatoes while Hassle sat importantly on the stool and inspected the other diners. Two switch engineers and a gaudy lady from Battle Row sat at one of the tables, laughing and wolfing flapjacks. There was the usual assortment of drifters sitting at the counter, drinking the cafe's bitter coffee and staring into space. In one of the plank booths sat three cowhands, their faces gray with trail dust, eating ham and eggs in grim silence.

"I can't go on much longer," one of the cowhands muttered, "without some sleep."

"Neither can Dutch," one of his pals said wearily.

"We don't even know that Dutch is *in* Oklahoma City."

"We know the pitchman's here. Where the pitchman goes, Dutch won't be far behind."

Hassle froze as he was about to fill his mouth with a forkload of steak and potatoes.

One of the cowhands yawned widely and rubbed his red-rimmed eyes. "I know it ain't for me to say," he told the older cowman who was obviously the boss of the outfit, "but I don't see why we don't leave it up to the law. They'll catch up to Dutch. He can't run much longer."

The older cowman glared at him. "It wasn't the law's horse that Dutch Rainey run off with," he said coldly. "It's my business, and nobody else's."

"The sorrel's dead," the second cowhand ventured. "Killin' Dutch won't get you the animal back."

The old cowman threw back his head and looked at the cowhands down his thin nose, as if he were looking down the barrel of a gun. "If word gets out that Matt Silver's the kind of man that'll set still while horse thieves ride off on company animals, why inside of a month I wouldn't have no livestock left." He was silent for a moment, his eyes almost closed. "Or you can look at it another way," he said grimly. "Settlin' up with Dutch Rainey is somethin' I've got to do. I won't rest till it's done. Like Dutch won't rest till he's killed that pitchman."

A piece of steak stuck in Hassle's throat. He began to cough violently. "I guess I ain't as hungry as I thought," he told the counterman, hurriedly counting out the right amount of silver. Before the cafeman could say anything, the boy had jammed his hat on his head and was out the door.

California Sam was sitting at a front table in the Lucky Frisco, happily dealing the cards as the other unhappy-looking players closely watched. "I got to talk to you," Hassle said, tugging at the pitchman's arm.

"Not now," Sam told him, smiling as he peeked at his hole card.

"It's important," Hassle insisted.

The players regarded the boy in annoyance. At last Sam shrugged his heavy shoulders in resignation. "All right, boy, but not till after I finish this hand."

They played the hand out in silence. A cowhand opened with two jacks. The other players called. Sam raised. The pile of chips in the center of the table grew steadily as more cards were out and bets in, the pitchman turned up a full house. "Looks like my lucky night, gents," he chuckled comfortably, adding chips to the already considerable stack in front of him. He turned to Hassle. "All right, boy, what is it?"

"It's gotta be private," Hassle said.

Sam smiled apologetically at the others. "This won't take a minute." He shoved back his chair and ambled toward the back of the saloon. "Boy," he said, on the verge of exasperation, "don't you know it's bad luck to interrupt a body when he's on a winnin' streak? What's the matter with you anyhow?"

"There's somebody out to kill you!" Hassle blurted. "Somebody by the name of Dutch Rainey. I heard it at the cafe."

The pitchman looked at his assistant as if the boy had suddenly grown a second head. "Son, you haven't been drinkin' anything stronger'n coffee, have you?"

"I'm tellin' you the truth! There was three cowhands at the cafe—or two hands and a boss cowman, I guess. The boss said his name was Matt Silver. They'd been on the trail a long time, from the looks of them. Best I could make out, they was after this Rainey for horse stealin', and they was lookin' for him in Oklahoma City because you *was* here."

"Boy," California Sam said with an enormous sigh, "that don't make no sense at all."

"I know it sounds loco, but it's what they said. The man called Dutch Rainey is lookin' to kill you. That's how they knowed they'd find him in Oklahoma City."

"Son," the pitchman told him with flagging patience, "I don't know anybody by the name of Dutch Rainey. I don't know anybody by the name of Silver. How do you know they was talkin' about me?"

"They said that Rainey was goin' to kill a pitchman."

"There you are!" Sam exclaimed, with an extravagant wave of dismissal. "The world's full of pitchmen. They was talkin' about somebody else."

"They was talkin' about you, I know it!"

Sam looked toward the table and nodded to his fellow poker players. "We'll talk about it some other time," he told Hassle. "When I ain't got so much to think about." He patted the boy condescendingly on the head and lumbered back to the game.

In a high state of frustration, Hassle went outside and sat on the steps of the saloon. He tried to tell himself that the pitchman was probably right. Probably the cowmen had been talking about somebody else. Probably he hadn't understood them right in the first place.

But deep inside, where his heart hammered anxiously, he knew that he was right. Somewhere in Oklahoma City there was a horse thief by the name of Dutch Rainey, and for reasons that Hassle could not imagine, he was bent on killing the pitchman.

Slumped dejectedly on the steps of the Lucky Frisco, Hassle watched the night drag to a ragged end. One by one the saloons along Bunco Alley closed their doors. The lights went out of second-story windows. The painted ladies vanished.

Hassle shivered. A false dawn appeared briefly in the eastern sky and then was gone. The big octagonal clock over the bar of the Lucky Frisco said four o'clock.

At four-thirty California Sam came out of the saloon smiling widely. "Looks like she's goin' to be a fine day!" he said rubbing his hands enthusiastically. "We've got us a bankroll, boy, a real bankroll!"

"You been thinkin' about what I told you?"

"What's that, boy?" the pitchman asked idly.

"About the man called Rainey that aims to kill you."

"Sure, I been thinkin' about it, and I decided it was just a young'un's imagination gettin' overworked. I wonder if that cafe's open; I could use some grub."

They walked down the silent street to the Santa Fe tracks, but the cafe was closed. Everything was closed. "Well," Sam sighed philosophically, "I guess I'll have to go to bed with a grumblin' belly." He brightened as they turned back toward Broadway. "Did I tell you how much I won in the game tonight?"

"No," Hassle said glumly. For one of the rare times in his life he was not especially interested in money.

"Four hundred dollars!" Sam told him proudly. "What do you think of that?"

Hassle stared at him. Probably if all the money he had

ever seen had been put together, it wouldn't have come to four hundred dollars. He squinted suspiciously and said, "How'd you do it?"

"Why boy," Sam grinned, "I swear I don't know what you mean!"

"Did you cheat?"

The pitchman managed to look mildly indignant. "Boy, you got the biggest imagination I ever come across. Look me in the eye; does old California Sam look like a man that'd cheat at cards?"

"Yes," Hassle muttered uneasily. "And I didn't like the looks of them other gamblers . . . There ain't no chance of them findin' out, is there?"

"I'm hurt, son," Sam said comfortably. "That you'd think such a thing about old Sam." They walked a short distance in silence, then he added thoughtfully, "I don't *think* there's any chance they'll catch on. Still, it's hard to tell about gamblers. Might be smart, at that, if we pulled out of Oklahoma City pretty soon."

"There's a southbound Santa Fe at six o'clock," Hassle said quickly. "I always wanted to see Texas."

"Well, now . . ." The pitchman's exuberance had settled down to a slow simmer. He wasn't actually worried, but if those gamblers went to the trouble to inspect the deck closely enough, Oklahoma City might not be such a comfortable place to be. As they tramped north on Broadway he began to imagine that the silent city was watching them. Over to the west somewhere a switch engine huffed in the Frisco freight yard. Sam decided that he liked the sound. It suggested far places, fresh adventures, a new group of suckers. Besides that, a moving target wasn't so easy to hit.

He grinned down at Hassle. "Might be you got a point, boy; wouldn't do to wear out our welcome in Oklahoma City. We'll just pack our grips and grab that southbound and have ourselves a look at Texas."

Hassle heaved a sigh of relief. When they turned in at

Mrs. Brent's he was walking with a new spring in his step. His anxieties melted. Somehow it didn't seem possible that anything very violent could happen at five o'clock in the morning. "You ever been to Texas?" he asked, swinging along at the pitchman's side.

"Sure I have, son. Fine people, Texans—great believers in the power of a strong physic . . ." Suddenly he pulled up, scowling deeply. "Somethin's wrong here. I never left a lamp burnin' in that room, did you?"

Hassle stared up at the orange square light. Suddenly he felt sweaty and sick. "It's that killer, Dutch Rainey!"

"Don't talk foolish, boy," Sam told him impatiently. "Would a killer sit up there in our own room, with the lamp burnin' bright?"

"Maybe it's the gamblers."

The pitchman shook his head. "They might of been poor poker players, but they wasn't fools." He put out his hand and moved Hassle to one side. "Stay behind me, boy. We'll take them stairs quiet and easy and have a look in the window."

They mounted the outside stairway with the care of tightrope walkers crossing a windy gorge. When they reached the top landing Sam leaned far over the railing and peered through the window. "Hell and damnation!" he groaned, turning back to the boy. "It's that redheaded pennyweighter again!"

"Rose?" Hassle broke into a wide grin.

They trooped into the dark hallway and threw open the door to the room. Rose was sleeping soundly on the pitchman's bed. The sight of her drawn face, waxy with exhaustion, pulled Sam up for a moment. She wore the lifeless gray print dress that Sam had bought for her before leaving Pond Creek; it made her look like a farm wife after a long day of looking after a demanding family.

Hassle touched her shoulder. "Rose? You all right?"

She opened her eyes and looked at him blearily. Suddenly

she smiled. "Of course I'm all right." She sat up on the edge of the bed and looked startled when she saw daylight bleeding through the morning darkness. "It's almost daylight!" she accused the pitchman angrily. "What do you mean keepin' this boy up till such an hour?"

"It was his own idea," Sam told her sourly. "Now maybe you'll tell me what *you're* doin' here. I haven't had time to buy more diamond stickpins, if that's what you're lookin' for."

Rose's eyes flashed with some of her old fire. "I guess I was actin' the fool, but I came here to save your hide. Do you know a hardcase cowhand called Dutch Rainey?"

Hassle made a sound of astonishment, but the pitchman silenced him. "No, I don't know him."

"Well . . ." Rose spread her arms in a gesture of helplessness. "He knows you. He bought some of your electric hair restorer and it might nigh took the scalp right off his head. He was so mad that he set out for Wichita to kill you."

Sam and Hassle listened with growing apprehension as Rose told the story in detail, as she had heard it in Pond Creek. "There's military and sheriff's posses lookin' for him," Rose said, winding up her tale of violence and murder. "But I don't think they'll find him."

"Why not?" Sam asked tonelessly.

"Accordin' to what's on the telegraph, he's got a busted leg and a bullet in his gut, and *that* hasn't stopped him. He's killed a sheriff's deputy, and a captain of cavalry, and maybe he even set the prairie fire that almost killed us. Still, nobody's been able to catch him. Looks like the only thing that's keepin' him alive now is the notion that he's goin' to kill you."

For a long while the pitchman sat hunched over wearily, saying nothing. In the distance he heard a train whistle hooting like a lost soul in the early morning. That would be the southbound to Texas. His passage to safety. But it was too late to catch it now.

He heard Hassle rattling on excitedly about the three cowmen in the railroad cafe, but the pitchman paid no attention. He was thinking about Dutch Rainey, and strangely, he was thinking about him without hostility or fear. It sounded insane that a man, because of a blistered scalp, could murder two men in cold blood, ride good horses to death and set prairie fires. But he knew that such things happened. There were doomed men in the world, and Dutch was one of them. And doomed men didn't care who they took down with them.

Suddenly the pitchman became aware of a ringing silence in the room. He looked up in alarm. Rose and Hassle were sitting in curiously frozen positions, their heads cocked in attitudes of intense concentration. Rose got up from the bed and went quietly to the window. "There's some men comin' up the walk," she said.

Sam's stomach took a breath-taking dive. "How many?"

"Four," Rose said quietly. "I don't much like the looks of them."

Sam got up and went to the window. One of the men carried a rifle, another a shotgun. Two had large revolvers buckled around their waists. Not a comforting sight in a town where the wearing of firearms was strictly forbidden by law.

Hassle made a small sound of dismay as he crowded in at the window. "It's the poker players!" He glared up at the pitchman. "You did cheat in that game, didn't you?"

"Son," the medicine man told him nervously, "all I did was put a few thumbnail marks on some of them cards. You couldn't hardly call that cheatin'."

"That's what *they'll* call it," Rose told him. "Is there some place you can hide till things simmer down?"

Sam couldn't think of any place. His mind was blank. All he could see was those four guns and the grimly determined faces of the men who carried them. "I'm done for," he said weakly. "I got a mighty strong notion that them four gents ain't in any frame of mind to listen to explanation."

"There's Mrs. Brent's root cellar," Hassle said.

This was welcome news to the pitchman. "Don't just stand there, boy, show me where it's at!" He turned to Rose. "Does Mrs. Brent know you're here?"

"She let me in last night." A wry little grin darted across her face. "I told her you was my husband."

The pitchman groaned. Hassle, with his nose pressed against the window, said, "They're openin' the gate. They're headed toward the front gallery." His eyes were wide with alarm. "Follow me," he told the pitchman. "I'll show you the cellar."

"You tell them somethin'," Sam said to Rose, as Hassle tugged him into the dark hallway. "Tell them I went to Texas. Tell them . . . anything."

In the pitchman's ears the four gamblers sounded like a troop of mounted cavalry as they tramped onto Mrs. Brent's front gallery and pounded on the door. "Move spry, boy! It's time we got ourselves out of here!"

They blundered down the dark hallway to the rear landing where Hassle shinnied expertly down the outside stairway, which was not a real stairway at all but a plain ladder nailed to the side of the house. The medicine man followed him down with reckless speed, landing in a bed of the landlady's petunias. He followed the boy across a yard cluttered with flower beds and cast-off furniture.

"Here it is," Hassle hissed, lifting a plank door. The pitchman could hear the gamblers talking to Mrs. Brent. He and the boy ducked quickly into the dark hole, pulling the door closed after them. "Godamighty, boy," Sam complained, "what kind of place is this, anyhow?"

"Root cellar," Hassle told him. "I come down here yesterday while you was sleepin' to get some stuff for Mrs. Brent. Look out for potatoes, they're all over the floor. Over against the wall are jars of jelly and peaches and things like that. The best place to hide is over here in the corner; there's some straw you can cover up with, if they happen to look for you down here."

"If they look down here," Sam told him hopelessly, "I'm done for, boy."

The pitchman struck a sulphur match and glumly surveyed the gravelike cellar. For some time he cocked his ear to the tin stovepipe that acted as a ventilator, but all he could hear was the mournful sighing of the wind. "Hell and damnation!" he complained bitterly. "How am I supposed to know what's goin' on up there?"

He stumbled over a small mountain of potatoes, blundered against a shelf of canned goods and at last sank down on a bed of straw in the corner of the cellar. But it was useless trying to get comfortable. The straw was full of potatoes and turnips.

A small eternity passed while they strained to hear what was going on outside. Then, for one heart-stopping moment, the door opened and a shaft of cold morning sunlight shot into the cellar.

It was Rose. "They're gone," she said, "but not for long."

The pitchman muttered something under his breath. "What did you tell them?"

"That you'd pulled out for Texas right after the game. They didn't believe it for a minute."

"Where are they now?"

"I ain't sure. Hassle, you come out of there. Mrs. Brent wants you to go to the store for her."

Reluctantly, the boy trudged up the dirt steps. "Stay where you are," Rose told the medicine man. "I'll see what I can find out." She let the heavy door fall with a crash.

Another eternity passed. The pitchman smoked his pipe while his imagination ran rampant. He began to think of the cellar as a grave. He heard footsteps moving back and forth endlessly overhead. He placed his ear to the stovepipe ventilator, but what he heard was not the sighing of the wind but the patient, malicious breathing of a savage enemy.

At last the door opened again and Rose came down the steps bearing a coal oil lantern. Sam was grateful for the light but uneasy about what it implied; more waiting. "How long have I been in this hole?" he demanded.

"Almost three hours. Hassle seen two of your gamblin' pals across the street keepin' a watch on the house. They must know you're here, but I guess they aim to wait till you show yourself before tryin' anything."

The pitchman was appalled, that he had been there less than three hours. It seemed to him that he had spent half a lifetime in this black hole, or at the very least, half a day.

"You'll have to set still till night comes," Rose told him. "Me and Hassle will figger out somethin' by that time."

She disappeared again and the door came down but this time the grave was lighted and, for a time, it wasn't so bad. But after a while the flickering light of the lantern became as disturbing as the darkness. Half-seen shadows darted along the walls. The pitchman began to imagine that something was moving in the pile of straw. On top of that, the strong smell of coal oil poisoned the already polluted air. He couldn't make up his mind which he hated worse, the lantern or the darkness.

At last Rose returned with a plate of food and some coffee. "They're still out here," she reported casually. "Still watchin' the house."

Distractedly, the pitchman took a piece of fried chicken off the plate and bit into it. He chewed for several seconds before realizing that it was excellent chicken, crusty on the outside, tender and moist on the inside. "Who cooked this? Not Mrs. Brent, I know."

"I did." She smiled faintly. "I'm workin' here now, for Mrs. Brent. I do the cookin' and she keeps the house."

Sam stared at her. "When did all this happen?"

"This mornin' when I helped with the breakfast." She

laughed self-consciously. "Hard to believe, ain't it? An old saloon girl like me workin' in a boardin'house." She shrugged. "Tell you the truth, it was all I could get. I looked for work in saloons, but they didn't want me. Then I gave myself a good studyin' in the lookin' glass, and I realized the saloons was right. I'm not a girl any more. I guess that's why I lost my head about gettin' married—even to a skunk like Alf Ritter. I was just sick of saloons and didn't know it."

Sam took another bite of chicken. "Well," he shrugged, "sometimes a thing goes sour—I guess workin' in saloons would, after a while."

She looked at him in a strange way. "What about pitchin' herbs to the natives? Does that go sour too?"

"Not if you're a pitchman." He tried some of the coffee and asked suddenly, "What was you doin' in my room this mornin'? It wasn't just to warn me about a crazy cowhand called Dutch Rainey."

She turned her head and for a moment the pitchman could have sworn that she was blushing. "No . . . that wasn't the real reason. The truth is I didn't have any place else to go. No job, no money—just the railroad ticket that you gave me in Pond Creek." She looked at him and smiled weakly. "You was good luck for me once—I thought maybe you'd be again."

"It must of been a big disappointment to you," he said dryly, "to catch me this time when I was out of diamonds."

Surprisingly, she failed to rise to the bait. "Well," the pitchman went on indifferently, "it don't matter now. Come nightfall me and the boy'll be headed out of the Territory."

For several seconds Rose was silent, but the pitchman could see that her mind was racing. "I don't want you to take Hassle with you," she said softly. "I want you to leave him here."

10

CALIFORNIA SAM lunged up from his pile of straw, dropping his chicken and overturning his coffee. "Woman, you're out of your head! Where could the boy go if he didn't go with me?"

"He could stay here at the boardin'house and earn his keep doin' chores for Mrs. Brent. I'd look after him best I could. He'd go to school and get an education like other kids, and maybe amount to somethin'."

Sam glared at her indignantly. "You call bein' a high pitchman *nothin'?*"

"Not for you. But I want Hassle to have somethin' better."

"Maybe you'd tell me why you're takin' such a big interest in the boy?"

She shrugged. "Back in Wichita we was kind of pals. We talked about things. Did you know he had it in mind to be a big man someday? Doctor, lawyer. No tellin' what he could be if he got the schoolin'."

"He never told *me!*"

"You was so busy teachin' him to be a pitchman that he never had a chance to tell you anything. Sam . . . Let him stay."

"Leave it to the boy," he said with a confident grin. "If he wants to stay, he can stay."

"You know he wouldn't do anything to hurt you. Someday it'll come to him that fleecin' yokels and riggin' poker games ain't such a big thing after all. But now he thinks you're a big man. He'll do whatever you tell him to do."

"The fair thing," he said stubbornly, "is leave it up to the boy. That's what I aim to do."

Something happened to Rose's eyes; they became remote and icy. "Let him stay, or I'll tell your poker playin' pals where you're hidin'."

The pitchman stared at her in alarm. In spite of her background of saloons and thievery he found it hard to believe that she would turn him over to a lynch mob. Still, it was impossible to tell about women. Redheaded women in particular. Redheaded pennyweighters especially. As they stood eying each other coldly, sizing each other up like two hungry coyotes over a fresh carcass, the cellar door lifted and Hassle said, "Mrs. Brent wants you in the kitchen, Rose."

Rose took up the empty plate and the overturned coffeepot and shot the pitchman a look that was full of knives. With no other word, she went up the steps and Hassle came down. "Did you know that Rose is workin' for Mrs. Brent now?" the boy asked.

"She told me."

"Mrs. Brent says she's the best cook she ever had. How did you like the chicken?"

"I liked it fine," Sam told him with a good deal of bitterness. "Set down, boy, I want to talk to you."

Hassle sat down on a mound of straw-covered turnips. "Talk about what?"

"Rose says you got it in mind to make an educated man out of yourself someday. How come you never told me about that?"

Was it the poor light, or was Hassle actually avoiding the pitchman's eyes. "That," he hedged with a shrug, "was just kid talk. A long time ago, up at Wichita."

"What do you think about it now?"

"I want to be a pitchman, like you."

With sudden savagery, Sam kicked a loose potato across the cellar floor. "A pitchman. Well, I guess that's all right—if you like bein' tracked from town to town by crazy killers like Dutch Rainey. If it pleasures you to hide in a hole like a rabbit, scared to show your face for fear a lynch mob will be waitin' to slip a noose around your neck. If the best thing you can think of to do with yourself is fleecin' yokels and riggin' card games, why I guess the life of a pitchman's about as good as any other."

The boy stared at him in surprise. "What're you talkin' about?"

"What I just told you—what it's like bein' a pitchman. A medicine man. A peddler, a hawker, a sharpshooter with more up his sleeve than just his arm."

"What's the matter with you?" Hassle asked in amazement.

"I don't know, boy." The medicine man shrugged and managed a watery smile. "Maybe it's Rose's cookin'. My stomach ain't used to digestin' anything softer'n bullets. It throws me out of kilter."

"You'll be all right tonight, won't you? We're headin' for Texas, ain't we?"

"Texas," the pitchman said. Suddenly he smiled. "Some of the most trustin' suckers in the world are Texans. Go back to the house, boy, and pack our grips. As soon as it's dark we'll be pullin' out of here."

"There's a night train headin' south at eight o'clock. I asked Mrs. Brent."

"Fine, fine," the pitchman told him. "Eight o'clock will be just right."

Around midafternoon the door opened and the hatchet face of Widow Brent peered into the gloom of her root cellar. "Mr. California Sam? Is that your name?"

"Yes ma'am," the pitchman told her, "that's what they call me."

She eased her way down the dirt steps and for some time stood looking at the medicine man as if he were a side of meat that she was thinking about cutting up. "Rose," she said at last, "told me that you and her are married. I know better, of course. Your kind don't ever get married. In a lot of ways you remind me of my late husband; he wasn't much good either."

"I'm sorry to hear that, ma'am," Sam told her.

"Rose tells me you're in bad trouble. She didn't say what kind, and I don't want to know. But you're free to stay here in my cellar till nightfall. After that, I'd feel easier if you left."

"Yes ma'am," Sam said meekly. "I aim to do just that. And I'm much obliged for all the help you've been."

"It ain't for you that I'm doin' it. I'm doin' it for Rose and the boy. Not for any muleheaded reason that might be occurrin' to you—I need a good cook, and Rose is willin' to work cheap. And there's plenty to do around a boardin'-house to keep a boy busy; he'll earn his keep."

"Yes ma'am," Sam said.

"You owe two dollars rent on your room. Three dollars, countin' today."

Sam peeled off three dollar bills and gave them to her. She inspected the money closely, and when she could find nothing wrong with it put it in her apron pocket. "I must say," she went on with a steel-trap smile, "that things have been lively since you and the boy moved into the room. There hasn't been so much doin' since my late husband passed on."

Sam grinned. "It'll be quieter tomorrow."

"I hope so. The late Mr. Brent was a trial to me, to his dyin' day."

After what seemed a long time later Rose opened the cellar door again and came down the steps. Hassle came behind her, lugging the pitchman's heavy grip.

"It looks all right," Rose said, helping the pitchman on with his buckskin jacket. "Hassle spotted two of your gamblin' pals in a wagon bed on the other side of the street. Two more are layin' back in a lilac bush at the corner of the front yard. If you cut across the back way you ought to make the railroad tracks without any trouble. I don't guess you've got a gun, have you?"

"A gun?" Sam recoiled at the thought. "I'd rather carry a pocketful of rattlesnakes. "Boy," he said to Hassle, "where's your grip?"

"Hassle ain't goin'," Rose said, her chin jutting defiantly.

The pitchman looked at the boy who shifted from foot to foot, knocking loose potatoes about on the dirt floor. "Is that right, son?"

". . . I guess so," the boy said, not looking him in the eye. "Rose and Mrs. Brent figger I'd be better off here in Oklahoma City than on the road with you. I guess maybe they're right."

"I see." The pitchman cleared his throat and gazed up thoughtfully at the roof of the cellar, but he couldn't think of anything to say. Somehow he had been looking forward to showing the boy the country as he himself had seen it as a young man. He's got a good head on his shoulders, Sam sighed to himself. I could of made a first-class pitchman out of him. I'd work up a good lecture for him. Get a professional writer to put it all down on paper, so he could learn it by heart. The boy's got natural flash; the yokels wouldn't stand a chance!

But all he said was, "Well, maybe Rose and Mrs. Brent are right. You stay here and get some schoolin'. Someday, if I feel the need of a educated man, I'll send you a telegram."

The boy grinned bleakly. Everybody seemed to run out of talk at the same time. After an uncomfortable silence, Sam picked up his grip and started up the steps.

"Keep on the north side of the house as you make for the street," Rose told him. "That'll put the house between you and the lilac bush."

The pitchman nodded. "I'll remember." As he started to walk off, she spoke again.

"Sam, you're doin' the right thing about the boy."

"I'm doin' what I said I'd do. He decided for hisself." He tucked his grip under his arm and squinted into the darkness. It looked like an easy sprint to the limits of Mrs. Brent's back yard and across the street to the Santa Fe tracks.

"Goodbye, Sam."

"Goodbye, Rose. It's been right interestin' knowin' you, I'll say that much." With a duck of his head he took a fresh hold on his grip and started jogging across Mrs. Brent's back yard.

Within a matter of seconds he was out of breath, huffing and wheezing like an old high-stack Baldwin locomotive. "Damnation!" he gasped, tripping over one of the landlady's cast-off chairs and sprawling on the hard earth. He lay there for a full minute getting his breath. If I ever make it to them tracks, he thought, it won't be by runnin'. It'll be walkin' slow and easy, standin' straight up like an honest native. He started to push himself upright when Hassle suddenly appeared out of a tangle of climbing roses.

"Godamighty, boy," the pitchman blurted, "you liked to scare the lights out of me! What're you doin' here anyhow? You're supposed to be back with the womenfolks."

"I don't want to stay with the womenfolks, I just told Rose that to save a fuss. I'm goin' with you." With an emphatic thump he placed his own grip beside the pitchman's.

"Are you now?" Sam said with a spreading grin. Somehow he no longer felt old and heavy. It seemed that new life surged in his hardening arteries as he and the boy regarded each other with self-conscious affection. "Well," the medicine man said, "if you've made up your mind, I guess you've made up your mind. So we better get started; we ain't goin' to catch that train settin' here."

"Bear a little more to the north," Hassle told him. He chuckled to himself. "I wonder how long them poker players are goin' to set out there watchin' the house for us."

"Long enough to let us catch that train, I hope," the pitchman said with feeling.

They stepped over the wire fence that marked the limits of Mrs. Brent's back yard, and Sam felt as if he were stepping out of a prison. He was free. Even the air tasted cleaner. He and the boy looked at each other grinning. In the distance they could hear a locomotive idling, with metallic clanking and occasional hissing, like some enormous beast dozing. "Well," the pitchman said with swelling confidence, "it won't be long now!"

The medicine man and the boy skidded down the clay embankment to the street. Then, as they were about to recover their grips, the sky seemed to crack open with stunning violence.

"Godamighty, boy!" The pitchman stood dumbstruck beside the road, staring at the flash of light. There was a second violent explosion, so nearby that it hurt his eardrums. Something went screaming past his head. "Hell and damnation! Somebody's shootin' at us with a rifle!"

Sam and Hassle threw themselves into the gully beside the road. "Boy, are you all right?"

"I'm all right. Who's that shootin' at us?"

"I never asked, and he didn't say."

Another tongue of fire stabbed at them, and a bullet slammed with sickening impact into the clay bank over the pitchman's head. The night that had seemed so quiet and peaceful was suddenly filled with alarming sounds. The shouting of excited men filled the night. The sound of pounding feet seemed everywhere.

Rifles from every point of the night began to blaze as Sam and the boy lay frozen on the gravelly bottom of the gully. Somewhere in the distance they could hear Rose McGee screaming.

Then, as suddenly as it had started, it stopped.

Someone called, "That's it! That's enough!" They heard footsteps coming toward them from the four points of the campus. They could hear men breathing hard with excitement. The cool night air was harsh with the smell of gunsmoke.

Someone called, "Does anybody see the medicine man or the boy?"

"Not yet," another voice called from nearby. "But here's the killer."

Three men with rifles crossed Broadway and made for the place where the shooting had started—one was a military officer, the others were uniformed policemen. "Son," California Sam said with deep-felt emotion, "you can take my word for it, there goes the two best-lookin' policemen I ever seen. You sure you're all right?"

"I think so." The two of them sat up in the gully and checked themselves over. A burly police sergeant came over to them, hunkered down by the edge of the gully and looked at them. He made sure the boy was all right, if a little shaky, then turned to the pitchman.

"You the medicine man called California Sam?"

Sam weakly admitted to the name.

The sergeant grinned. "This is your lucky night, Sam. Another minute and that lobo would of killed you sure. He must of hated you plenty to go through all he went through just for a chance to kill you."

Several of the lawmen had rolled the body down to the shoulder of the road and were looking at it. "Who was it?" the pitchman asked at last.

"Hardcase cowhand by the name of Rainey. Best we can tell, he was just settin' up there by Mrs. Brent's fence waitin' for you to show yourself." He shook his head in wonder. "Yes sir, he must of hated you plenty. Knee twisted out of shape, and a bullet hole in his right side, but that never stopped him. Trailed you all the way from Wichita, I hear."

Sam wet his dry lips and cleared his throat. "Do you know why?"

The sergeant laughed. "I ain't sure I got the story straight. Somebody said it was on account of some salve you sold him. It don't seem like much to kill over, does it?"

Shaken more than he wanted to admit, the pitchman leaned back against the clay bank and tried to collect his thoughts. "Salve," he said in a stunned voice. "Would somebody set out to kill a man on account of a thing like that?"

"This one did," the sergeant told him cheerfully. "Well, set still a minute and get yourself together. Pretty soon the other lawmen'll want to talk to you."

Hassle and the pitchman followed the policeman's advice and rested in the gully until the hammering in their chests became less frantic. "Well," the boy said finally with a weak grin, "there's one thing about it, anyhow. Them poker players won't be botherin' you for a spell, with all these policemen around."

The pitchman merely grunted and wondered how much time they had to catch that train out of the Territory. In the background he could hear Rose McGee anxiously calling for Hassle, but he didn't feel up to do anything about it.

After a while he stopped a passing sheriff's deputy and asked, "If you boys knowed where the killer was all this time, would you mind tellin' me why you sat out there and let him shoot at me and the boy before doin' anything about it?"

The lawman grinned good naturedly. "We didn't know where he was, we just guessed he'd be trailin' you, like he's been doin' ever since you left Wichita. So we kept an eye on you, figgerin' sooner or later Rainey would show hisself."

"I see. What if Rainey had killed me first?"

"That," the deputy said with a shrug, "is a chance we had to take."

"A chance *they* had to take," the pitchman muttered when the deputy had gone. He looked at Hassle thoughtfully. "Boy, I don't mind tellin' you, all this do-si-do has made me a mite nervous. Set here a minute. There's somethin' I want to see about." He picked up his grip and walked heavily toward the group of lawmen.

For some time he stood looking down at the still form of Dutch Rainey. The features of the dead face were still contorted. Even in death, Dutch seemed overcome with rage. The pitchman shook his head slowly from side to side. A sudden light flared as one of the possemen struck a match and lit a cigar. For a moment Sam saw that the dead man's scalp was cracked and peeling, but it didn't look much worse than a bad sunburn. "I don't know," the medicine man said shakily to no one in particular, "I just don't know."

"Loco," one of the lawmen said with admirable self-assurance. "Plain loco."

"I guess," the pitchman sighed.

The sheriff's deputy who was in charge of the posse took Sam to one side and asked him questions, but there wasn't much that the pitchman could tell him. He couldn't even remember seeing the dead man before. "Well," the deputy said finally, "it don't make any difference now. He's dead, and that finishes it."

"Is it all right if I go now? I was aimin' to catch the eight o'clock from the Santa Fe depot."

"It's all right with me. Like I say, he's dead. That finishes it."

The pitchman lingered only for a moment, for in the back of his mind he was beginning to think again about those four poker players. He stood there in the midst of the commotion, his face long and a little sad. He thought about calling to Hassle. But he didn't do it.

Like a man standing on the outside watching through an open window, he watched Rose McGee skid down the embankment and rush to Hassle. It was all the indignant boy could do to keep from being pawed and kissed by the agitated female.

"Well," Sam thought in a burst of generosity, "I guess there's worse things than gettin' kissed by a female." He grinned crookedly and lifted his hand just a little. "So long, boy."

But Hassle didn't hear him. He was too busy trying to fend off Rose McGee's motherly attentions.

"What was that you said?" asked the deputy.

"Nothin'," the pitchman told him with a watery smile. He dug out his corncob pipe and lit it. He picked up his grip and walked into the night.

Not until he was buying his ticket from the night operator did he discover Rose's note in the pocket of his buckskin jacket. For a moment he wondered how it had got there—then he remembered how Rose had so helpfully held his coat for him as he was preparing to leave Mrs. Brent's root cellar.

Dear Sam (the note began) *I don't want you to think I steal as a regular thing so I write this note. I'll pay it back, and the diamond stickpin too. As soon as I get it, if you'll let me know where you're at. But I need it for Hassle. Schoolbooks and clothes cost money, and there ain't much*

I'll be makin' at the boardin'house. I just don't want you to think I don't aim to pay it back, because I do. Rose McGee.

The note had been slipped into the pocket that had held his five hundred dollars. With shaking hands the pitchman counted what was left of his roll.

"How far," he asked the operator in a grim voice, "will fifty-four dollars and twenty-five cents take me?"

The operator, with the air of a man who has been asked everything, thumbed through his fare book and said, "Stoneville, Texas."

Stoneville. Somehow it had a quiet, peaceful ring to it.

"Stoneville will do fine," the pitchman said, shoving the money under the grill. The important thing was to get out of Oklahoma City before his poker-playing friends tracked him to the depot.

The distant blast of the eight o'clock's whistle sounded mournfully in the night, but it was a welcome sound to California Sam. He pocketed his ticket and went outside to wait in the deepest shadows he could find.

Stoneville.

A good, solid name, and no doubt populated by good, solid natives. California Sam could close his eyes and almost see them, their trusting faces turned up to him, all eagerness to hear about the lone white hunter who had dared to invade the sacred mountains of the Savage Wa-Hoe Indians . . .